MURDER COVE

A.M. Holloway

Your Book Company

eBook ISBN: 9781956648065

Paper ISBN: 9781956648072

Library of Congress Control Number: 2022901062

Printed in the United States of America.

Chapter 1

The box still rests in the same spot. No one has bothered to shift it or look inside in years. I reached high above my head and jammed my fingers in the handholds. It turns out to be more of a struggle than expected, but I somehow haul it to my desk. My knife has no problem slitting the tape, sealing the contents inside. Once I lifted the lid, dust mites flew at record speed.

As I stare at the evidence in the box, I get a tingle of excitement and sadness. The evidence is from my dad's only unsolved case. This case has tugged at my heart for years, always in the back of my mind. Years ago, I decided I would solve it for my dad, but I couldn't bring myself to look at it until now. This box holds too many memories, but the time is right with everything that has happened in my life over the last few months.

Pictures from the box adorn the murder board in my office. I begin with the victim's picture, front and center. His name is Clement Locke. He was sixty-one years old at the time of death eight years ago. Clement owned and operated the cleanest pawn store I've ever seen. As a young child, I bought toys from him, and Dad always said I could count on Clement. His store was always open except on Sundays, Thanksgiving and Christmas Eve, and Christmas Day. Those are special days, as God gave them to us for a reason. I can still hear him say that to anyone questioning his operating hours.

An unknown subject beat Clement to death with a hammer and left him for dead in his pawnshop parking lot. I remember when my dad, as Sheriff, answered the call to Clement's. It took every bit of willpower he had not to shed a tear because that was the day this county's heart broke when news spread about Clement's death. It still hurts to see the pictures.

The hammer was still in the evidence bag. I glanced at the tag, and dad was the last one to sign it. My thumb rubs across the card. It still bothers me to this day every time I see dad's signature at the Sheriff's Office. Next, I pull the crime scene pictures from their pouches, and after I put them in order from the area of death, I tack them to the board. Several photos remain on my desk as duplicates, so I move them to the side. Then I retrieve the pictures of the store's interior and glance through the stack, selecting the most prominent ones for display. The crime scene guys went all out for Clement's scene. As a result, there are hundreds of photos between the inside of the store and the parking lot.

Clement's store stood alone on a two-lane road on the outskirts of town. He built the structure out of concrete blocks and wood. It withstood the weather and time, but it couldn't survive the murder of its owner. Over the years, businesses have moved in and out of that building, but no one saw success after Clement.

As I thumb through the remaining interior photos, something my dad stated about this case was, "I can't figure out what should stand out." Thinking back on that, I'm not sure what he meant by that statement or why I remembered it. Was something missing from the shop that no one noticed? Did it have to do with Clement?

With the pictures tacked to the board, I sat in my dad's leather desk chair and spun around until I faced the board. I started with the center picture, then moved outwards on each side. Without reading the file, I recalled there were no witnesses to the deed, and Clement did not have security. He did, however, have a mirror tucked into the store's corner. The mirror afforded him an ample view of the store. Someone busted the front door lock of the store, leaving the deputies to believe it was a robbery gone wrong. Luckily for the Sherriff's Office, Clement kept meticulous records of his purchases and sales. If he didn't feel the deal was legit, he sent you packing on down the road.

With the evidence littering my desk, I set up a six-foot plastic table in the corner of my office, giving me space to move the items. I glanced at the hammer, knowing there were no prints on it, but if you look closely, fingerprint dust remains. I wondered how someone could beat another human being to death with a hammer. The killer is brutal, for sure. Clement's store keys are in a separate bag with evidence of dried blood. He held the keys in his hand when the beating took place, and his blood-soaked clothes were in another container. Again, the crime lab found no trace of evidence on them. "Has technology advanced enough to find something now?" I muttered to myself while I wrote a note on my pad.

As I studied the table and the murder board, I noticed more photos than physical evidence. Whoever killed Clement knew his schedule. The murder couldn't have happened at a better time of day for the killer. It was strange one of Clement's friends wasn't there to walk him out. Sometimes, Clements' friends hung out in the store while Clement worked.

Anyway, I'll spend many hours going through his inventory and comparing that to the photos. Dad never mentioned Clement's inventory, so I'm unsure if he made comparisons. He might have followed another lead and never had time to return to it. Who knows what happened, but I'll go through it all.

Once I reviewed the files, I'm ready to begin the investigation. Dad's file with his suspect list is at the bottom of the stack, and I plan to leave them there. At least until I gather my own suspects, then I might see how they compare.

File folders litter the bottom of the box, and Dad labeled each folder for easy reference. The inventory list is in a three-ring binder with the newest pages on the top. Clement was an exceptional businessman for someone who never finished school. He printed his records in perfect script.

Time flew by today because the evidence box engrossed me in something that I had somewhat dreaded. My assistant, Maggie, looked into my office and waved her hand as she headed home for the night. "Have a great weekend, Maggie." I waved my hand in the air.

"You too, Sheriff. Don't work all night." Maggie says with a glint in her eye.

The sounds in the Sheriff's Office grew dim as people left for the day. I glanced around my office, wondering if I should call it quits too, and pick it up tomorrow. However, since nothing waited on me at home, I might as well get some time in on this inventory. Just as I reached for the inventory binder, my cellphone rang.

"Sherriff Steele," I answered. Seconds later, a smile spreads across my face as I listened to Bud tell me how much he missed me. The last few months gave me a new lease on life. I found a sister I knew nothing about, and I met Bud, both during a serial murder case.

"Things are moving along for Lana and me on our transfer to Atlanta. It might take a month, but we'll be in Georgia within the next week." Bud offers, adding a tinge of excitement in his voice.

"Bud, that is outstanding. I hope the FBI didn't give you and Lana a hard time about moving away. I'm ecstatic and can't wait to have you here. Like we discussed, traveling is still part of your job, and we can handle it." My hand keeps the binder closed while I speak with Bud. He can tell when I'm multitasking, and I do that often.

"Are you still at the office, Jada? It's Friday. If you have nothing pressing, go home and rest. I'll call you later. Love you, Jada."

"I love you too, Bud. Talk later." I place my cellphone back in my pocket, so I don't leave it lying on the desk, which I have done before.

Glancing at the murder board, what will Bud think when he sees this? Will he be mad at me for opening this investigation? I'll explain my reasons when I see him. It's always better to tell him in person.

An enormous sigh escaped as I opened the binder, willing my nerves to settle. It doesn't take long to figure out Clement's inventory process. Every purchase he made has a date, time of day, the seller with contact information, and item description. The same information applies to every sale. Based on the item description, I should be able to match the item in a picture. The process begins with the first item in his inventory. An hour later, and so far, so good, I have spotted each item in a picture and notated it with the picture number. This is time-consuming but worth it. With the number of things at Clement's store, the murder may result from the property. Not a person.

My stomach growls, reminding me I skipped supper again. At 9:00 pm, I dropped the red pencil on my desk and stood. My body needs liquid and food. I tell myself this is secondary to anything, but it's hard to let go.

As soon as I slid into the cruiser, I radioed dispatch and advised my status would be home. The last few weekends have been busy with domestic violence calls because summer brings out fights and disagreements. Since some people can't handle the heat and humidity in South Georgia, they get testy. However, the weekend forecast calls for rain bands coming up from a tropical storm in the Gulf. Hopefully, this will hinder the calls this weekend, giving the deputies a reprieve from activity.

Bud and Lana can't make it home for the weekend. Their transfer papers didn't come through yet, so they will help their current team in Louisiana. With luck, they should be in Georgia next week. It disappointed me I couldn't see him, but that left me time to work on Clement's file, and that I did.

With the weekend behind me, I entered the Sheriff's office lot. By the looks of the spaces, everyone beat me to work today. Being the Sheriff, I don't have a specific time to be at the office, but I try to be here by eight. Mornings are the best time to handle stuff without needing my undivided attention. The day sometimes turns chaotic.

Maggie brings a few phone messages from the weekend and updates me on staff. We have one deputy out for the birth of a child due today. One down before the day even starts. The city council met last week and approved the request for an additional deputy, but I haven't received notification from anyone giving me the authority to hire. I jotted a note to follow up. This needs to happen sooner rather than later.

The weekend reports sit waiting for me to review them, but my mind isn't on it. We had a traffic accident, a theft from the movie theater, and a peeping tom call. Overall, the weekend was slow, making me wonder what was coming. Anytime a weekend is this quiet, it's usually a precursor to something dire. My mind travels to Bud and Lana, wondering how they are faring.

I glanced at the murder board, and then the inventory list. As I picked up the red pencil, I found an item on the list. For the next few hours, I continue working on Clement's inventory. During this time, I spot a diamond ring missing from the jewelry case photo. This is an exciting turn of events. The diamond ring sounds gorgeous and not the usual run-of-the-mill ring from the big box stores. I wonder if an independent jeweler designed and made this ring? If so, which one? The likelihood of our jeweler making this ring is slim, but I'll ask.

The phone rings on my desk, and I cringe every time I listen to it. It is the most annoying ring possible, but I can't replace it because it belonged to my dad. He loved that old phone. One day I will do something about it.

"Steele," I answered the phone with authority, knowing the caller wasn't calling to check on me.

"This is Deputy Taylor, Sheriff. We need you at the boat ramp off Harper Road. A fisherman found a male floating in the lake. I've verified the victim is on our side of the county."

"On my way, Taylor. Did you call for a boat?"

"Tuttle is bringing the boat. I called him first, knowing how slowly he drives while pulling a boat." Taylor chuckles when he remembers the first time Deputy Tuttle hauled a boat. He couldn't figure out how to keep the boat in between the lines on the road. They still rib Tuttle about it.

"See you soon." I close the computer, glance at the inventory once more, and lock my door on the way out.

Chapter 2

Sirens blare as I maneuver through afternoon traffic. I wasn't in too big a hurry to see a water death. They are the worst. Lana shares the same sentiment as me on water death. The memory floats through my mind as Lana describes the girls found in Mobile Bay. A serial killer shot them and dumped their bodies. While driving, I prayed that the body drowned instead of being murdered.

I followed Deputy Tuttle and the boat into the lot. He parks it with practiced ease. I waved my arm out the window and gave him a thumbs up for the great show. Once we gathered at Deputy Taylor's car, he shared his information, which isn't much. He points, then states, "The fisherman over there is the one that found the guy. He told us where to look, so as soon as we can get the boat in the water, we'll go get him."

"Let's go. The day isn't getting any longer, and I don't want to lose what light we have left." I told the guys as I texted Bud, letting him know my status since he said he would call me this evening. "Hey, Taylor, did you remember to let Lana know your status for the night?"

His face turns a bright red. "I'll do it right now. Thanks, Sheriff. This relationship stuff is hard." He shook his head as he plucked his cell phone from his pants pocket and fired off a text.

I didn't want to admit it, but Taylor was right. This relationship is work. I've never had to check in with anyone since dad died. My relationship with Bud grew fast during the serial killer hunt. The same happened for Lana and Taylor. We still talk about finding love during a scary time for us all. We almost lost Lana to the killer, and it brought us to our knees. I never want to experience anything like that again.

The boat bobs on the lake as small waves break at the boat launch. Deputy Tuttle calls my name, and when I turn to face him, everyone sits in the boat but me. The memories flooded back, and I couldn't stop the train. "Show us the way, Taylor. Tuttle, did you bring the grappling hooks?"

Tuttle points to the back of the boat, and there lay two bags. Both bags hold the ropes and hooks we use for dragging the lake. Thank goodness we don't use them often. I gave him a nod, as if saying thanks. The boat ride was bumpy. People have taken to the lake on a hot summer day. We watched people on skies and tubes as we rounded the bend in the lake. I noticed our proximity to the neighboring county.

Our county borders the lake along with two other counties on opposing sides. The state's main interstate dissects the lake twice. The lake on our side only has Corp of Engineer property with a few campgrounds and two boat ramps, while the other two counties have residential housing, a golf course and a kid's park. I snapped pictures with my phone for later as we turned into the cove.

"Here's the spot, Sheriff, but I don't see a body."
Taylor looks around the cove with eyebrows
bunched together.

"If the fisherman is legit, there's a body here
somewhere. Pull out the ropes and start dragging.
Boat traffic could have forced the body further into
the cove."

Tuttle cut the boat engine and started working with
the trolling motor. The guys unleashed the ropes and
hooks as we moved a little closer to shore. They
pulled up tree branches, a tackle box, and an old
plastic float. But they never recovered a body.

The guys looked at me as I pondered on our next
move. "Do we have the fisherman's phone number?
I'd like a word." Between the heat and these flies, I
felt nauseous, and I'm uncertain why. Usually, I
don't get motion sickness.

Taylor produces the fisherman's contact information
from his bag. He passes it over as he and Tuttle
continue dragging. Dragging a lake is time
consuming because of the current. A strong current
like today could take a body anywhere in this lake.
Our hope is a tree or outcropping of rocks snagged
our body.

While I was on the phone with the fisherman, he
described a tree branch sticking out of the water
several yards into the cove, and because of its
position in the water, it's recognizable. As the call
ended, I motioned to the guys to move towards the
curve in the cove.

"The fisherman described the tree branch over there. It's his favorite fishing spot. Or it was. He doesn't think he can fish there again after what happened."

Tuttle steers the boat over to the branch, and the guys throw the ropes and hooks overboard. Within ten minutes, they hoist a male corpse into the boat. The hooks have a hold on his right thigh, and the other one pierced his body on his back left shoulder area. Once they wrestle him onto the boat floor, Tuttle gasps and steps back. "What is that?" He points to the man's hand.

Taylor and I walked around to the man's back and looked at his hands. Someone tied his hands behind his back before throwing him into the lake. My guess is he was already dead when he hit the water because of the dime-sized hole in his forehead. As my eyes take in the visual, I realize the man is holding someone else's hand. He died back-to-back with a female, and somehow her hand remained in his when her body became separated. But where is the female, and how did she lose a hand?

All of us shake our heads as we come to terms with our situation. "Should we continue dragging, Sheriff? We're missing another person."

"I don't know about you, but I can't ride around in this blistering sun with this body at my feet. The odor is already affecting me." I stated as I waved my notebook in front of my face.

Taylor and Tuttle agree as Taylor pulls his cell phone from his pocket. He dials the medical examiner and asks for a pickup at the boat ramp. "We'll deliver this one and start over. I assumed that the other body should be close, but then again, it's uncertain how far they floated with the boat traffic."

We sat in the boat, waiting for the medical examiner to arrive while discussing strategy. They agree to continue the search until dark and make other arrangements if no one recovers the body. We were quiet as we studied the female hand with her manicured nails painted a light lilac and a silver ring on her middle finger. There are no tattoos or markings on the hand to help with identification. Something sharp separated her hand a little way past the wrist. There is no visible skin tearing, just a clean cut.

We heard the medical examiner's wagon back down the boat ramp and spin tires in the dampness. Once they gained traction, the driver pulled up a few feet. Harold is the driver, and he's been with the medical examiner's office for fifteen years. Waving at us, he opened the back door and pulled out a body bag.

"Sheriff, Guys, sorry to have to see you like this. What did you find?" Harold questions.

I explained our find and the female hand. Harold's eyebrows lifted when I mentioned the hand. "Have you ever seen that, Harold, or have we given you a first?" I poked at him, as I've known Harold since I was a kid. He's a few years older and like an uncle to me.

"This is a first, Sheriff. You say the deceased is holding another person's hand. Let me look for myself, not that I don't believe you." Harold winks at me.

Harold climbs into the boat with us, walks around to the man's back, and lifts the guy's shirt. "You are correct, Sheriff. He is holding a female hand. That's an awful clean cut on her arm. You're looking at a boat propeller, if I had to guess, but we'll confirm when we get her on the table. Do you have the rest of her?"

"No, we don't. We were sitting here working on a strategy for recovery."

"The only strategy I see is you have to find her. She's out there somewhere." Harold stated while unzipping the bag. "Another item of interest, based on decomp and odor, your man here has been floating about three to four days." The men load the man into the bag and help Harold slide him into the wagon. Harold glances back at me and says, "I'll call when I have more. It'll be in the morning. Doc James was working on one when I got your call." We watched as he pulled away from the ramp.

We settled back into the boat when my phone rang. "Hi, Bud. I'm with Taylor and Tuttle. We're dragging the lake for a female victim. I'll be home after dark unless we find her in the next little while. Call me later." I side with Taylor on this relationship thing. Bud always wants my whereabouts at all times, and that's a little cumbersome. Neither of our jobs allows for a regular workday. So when the call comes, he must drop whatever he's doing and travel to unknown destinations. When I look up, Taylor stares at me.

"What? Bud called. What are we waiting for? Let's go back to the same cove and start dragging again." I said as I ran my fingers through my hair, forcing myself to tie another ponytail. Taylor sees the call flustered me.

No one spoke on the ride back to the cove. We searched the water's edge for any signs of a body. All we have to go on is a hand. We have no clothing, ideas, or hair color. She could be anywhere in this lake, and that is a lot of water to search for.

"Guys, if Harold suggested the man was in the water for three days, the female wouldn't be floating by now, right?"

The guys look at me, and Taylor speaks up, "if I remember, bodies float five to eight days after death. That's how long it takes for the gases to form in the body. So, we might have another two days before she pops up somewhere. If a body floats without all extremities."

"Ugh. I was afraid you would say that. The image of the girl's hand clouds my judgment. Who would shoot two people, tie them together, and toss them in the lake? They must have made someone mad over something." I stated, more to myself than anyone, as I rubbed my temples, hoping to stave off a headache.

Deputy Tuttle powered up the boat, and we headed back to the lake cove, where the fisherman discovered the male subject. There were a few hours of daylight remaining, so we had to hurry. Upon our return to the cove, a cabin cruiser set anchor in the middle, preparing to stay for the evening. I flashed my badge at the boat owner and explained our situation.

"This is a free country, Sheriff, and I may stay here and watch you drag the lake." The man exclaimed with his chest puffed outward. His passenger didn't seem as excited as he was to see a dead person. She tugged on his t-shirt and whispered something in his ear. He huffed and puffed, then relented. We watched as he brought his anchor on board and pulled out of the cove. The boat owner never said a word on his way out.

Taylor shook his head, "Some people just don't get it, do they, Sheriff?" He unwraps our hooks.

"No, they don't. He tried to impress his girl, but he failed to ask if she wanted to see a dead person. For most people, that's a turnoff." I chuckled as I recalled the passenger's expression when I mentioned the dead body floating under their boat.

We threw the lines into the water, then we took turns pulling the ropes. It's exhausting work. By dusk, we had not located the girl. We stowed the ropes and hooks in their bags and made our way to the ramp.

"Guys, go home and rest tonight. We might have a long, hard day tomorrow. I'll call DNR for their help too. We can cover twice the space with two boats dragging." I pleaded with my deputies, as they were not the ones to give up on anything. As I climbed out of the boat, my shoulder gave me a fit. The muscles in my right shoulder tensed and wouldn't let go as a tennis ball-sized knot formed at the base of my shoulder blade. I rubbed it on the way to the cruiser, knowing it would take more than rubbing to loosen the knot.

Old injuries have a way to creep back into one's body. I thought my shoulder had healed, but after the strenuous work at the lake, it's apparent that didn't happen. My doctor gave me exercises to do at home. If I'm lucky, I can find the instructions again.

Dispatch was on the radio when I climbed into my vehicle. "Sheriff Steele. Repeat transmission."

The dispatcher requested my status. I complied while rubbing my shoulder. "What's up, Trudy? Do I need to stop in at the office?" Sometimes this girl beats around the bush before spilling the news.

"The media are here, and they want a report." She said in a rush.

"Tell them it will be tomorrow afternoon before I have something to say and send them home. I'm going home too." I placed the mic in the holder and started the car. Then Bud called to tell me he misses me. That one call improved my day.

Once I got home, I stripped off my smelly clothes and stepped into a scalding shower, hoping to ease the tension in my shoulder. It's enough that I can raise my arm above my head without too much pain. After completing a few shoulder stretches, I searched for a notepad and pen.

I jotted notes on everything that transpired today. Note-taking is a habit I picked up from my dad. The boat in the cove struck me as odd, but doubtless, it had anything to do with the body. But still strange. I described the man's body and the girl's hand. Someone's children are dead, and they don't have a clue.

My cellphone rings in my pocket. I snatch it out because it's never good if the phone rings at night. "Steele."

"Sheriff, Doc James here. The post-op is complete for your floater. I'm waiting for confirmation on the identification, and I should have it tomorrow. The man suffered a gash at his lower back and across his left hip. It appears a boat propeller sliced the female's hand from her body, creating a gash in the guy. The good news is the damage occurred post-death."

"That is good news, Doc. Did you restore the fingerprints on either victim?" I questioned, while writing notes.

"The process has begun, and it will finish overnight. Check with me in the morning, Sheriff. Were you able to locate the female today?"

"No. We recovered no one after the male subject. Hoping for better results tomorrow. Thanks for calling, Doc." The call ended, and I wrote a few notes and reminders for myself, then I fell asleep.

The following day started early. I had failed to eat supper last night, and my stomach growled so loudly that I must stop for food before meeting Taylor and

Tuttle at the boat ramp at seven. Little did I know, a fog rolled in overnight. When I reached the boat ramp, the lake was invisible. The sun poked through the fog, creating a brilliant shine on the water, which was creepy and beautiful at the same time.

My deputies pulled into the lot as I stood on the bank watching the battle between sunshine and fog. Tuttle backed the boat into the water while Taylor maneuvered it to the dock. Once Tuttle joined me, we jumped onto the boat deck and started our day.

With the fog, our pace was slow, so I updated the guys on Doc James' call. The fingerprints interested them, and the post-death damage to the female. "I'll call Doc James later this morning and see if the prints are back. The identification might help with the female information too." "Are you thinking the male and female were friends?" Tuttle asks with an eyebrow raised.

"I have no reason not to think they were friends. Why else would they be together? They were witnesses to something, or they partook in some wrongdoing. Either way, they were familiar with each other."

Both guys nodded in agreement. So many ideas ran through my head about why they were in the lake. It could be an argument over a person, drugs, or money. The boat glides into the cove, and we scan the shoreline for our female. We find nothing, so we throw the ropes and hooks again, starting at the back of the cove. In our discussion, we agreed to drag the cove before moving into open water. It will take all day to search this cove because it is so large and has multiple areas underwater that can harbor a body.

I continuously check my phone, waiting for Doc James and DNR to return my call. I would love for DNR to help drag the lake because it would cut down our search time since I have two deputies, not on road patrol. And that makes the other deputies work harder. I'll be glad when I can hire a new deputy. The ads for the paper and radio are ready for publication.

Taylor struggles to lift a rope, so Tuttle joins him. "It's hooked onto something. It might be a rock or tree under the water. This cove is where people drop their dead Christmas trees for fish habitats."

"Interesting. I've learned something new today, Taylor. At least they do something good for the lake." I reached over and tugged at the rope, too. "The rope isn't moving. Can we move the boat a little and see if the hook will release its hold?"

Tuttle gets back on the trolling motor and jostles us about a bit as he pulls alongside the rope. I peered into the murky water, trying to glimpse the issue, but it was more profound than I could see. "I see nothing, guys. Let's pull from the other side and see if we can get it to release."

Another minute and Tuttle has us lined up to yank on the rope. Taylor and I worked on the rope and finally, "Do we have another rope and hook in the bag? This could take all day trying to release the hook, and it's not worth the effort. We'll buy another to replace it. Unless someone wants to take a swim." I glance over at Tuttle and Taylor. Neither one made eye contact with me, and no one wanted to swim with a dead body.

My phone rings and the caller ID made my heart skip a beat. "Sheriff Steele." I listened as the DNR officer explained they were launching their boat now. Then I had the pleasure of letting him know our location.

"We have help on the way. Drop the rope and grab another one. I'll send DNR to the cove opening while we continue in the back. Surely, we'll find her before we meet in the middle."

The rest of Tuesday is uneventful. Neither we nor the DNR officer located our female victim. Doc James called around lunchtime, and our deceased male is Tucker Stranton. I recognized the name, but I can't remember where. I'll check our records when I return to the office.

"Our day ends here, and we'll start fresh tomorrow morning. Let's stop and speak with DNR on our way out." I instructed. We gather our belongings and approach the DNR boat.

"We're calling it a day. Thanks for your help today, even though we didn't find her. We covered a lot more territory with you here."

"Thanks, Sheriff. We'll join you tomorrow. If she's down there, tomorrow is the day."

"I'm banking on that statement, McAlister. Have a good evening."

As I turned around for my seat, Tuttle sped up, and Taylor grabbed my arm before I met the water.

"Tuttle, are you in a hurry?" I screamed over the boat motor. He's never driven this fast before.

Chapter 3

He didn't turn around and acknowledge my statement, either. What got into him? Did we make him mad? Taylor and I shared a glance and a shoulder shrug.

Once Tuttle sided up to the boat dock, he faced us and said, "I remember Tucker, the victim. I was new to the force when we arrested him on drug charges. He's about my age. It took me a while to place him, but I did it." Tuttle looks triumphant at his admission.

"Thanks, Tuttle. You've never driven the boat so fast before. We didn't understand what was wrong with you." Taylor states.

Now that we settled that issue, I stated, "You two go home. I'll stop by the office and pull Tucker's record. Perhaps we have personal information in his file that might help with the female's identity. If I count correctly, the female will float in the next two days. Tomorrow is Wednesday, and it will be our last day on the lake. Two deputies are out of the office on Thursday for firearms training. I need you two back on the road."

Taylor and Tuttle steal a glance from the other and agree with the Sheriff. Once they load the boat onto the trailer, the guys climb into the truck and pull away from the lot. I lean against my car and stare at the lake. Where is she? Lake traffic diminished from Monday. If the current took her away, how far would she have traveled? I can't stand knowing a body is in the lake with family members left in the dark.

Stopping at the office turned out to be a mistake. Maggie piled messages onto my desk by the dozens, covering the desktop. Everyone seeks information on the body. If we haven't recovered the female tomorrow, I'll provide a news conference Thursday morning. That should satisfy them for a minute.

I handled the urgent items at the office, along with Tucker's records. We arrested him in the past on several charges involving drugs. At one point, we thought he might be a distributor, but we proved nothing. Why would someone kill him and then toss him into the lake if he hasn't been in trouble with the law for a while?

As I stood to leave for the day, I glanced back at the murder board. Clement stared back at me. My gut clenched, and I sat down for just a minute. I perused the inventory for over an hour, locating more items in the pictures. My phone rang, and my heart skipped a beat listening to Bud tell me his transfer papers are due tomorrow.

"Bud, I can't believe it's happening. You're moving to Georgia. How soon can you move?" Sweat beaded up on my upper lip, and my hands turned clammy as I waited for an answer. This whole relationship thing bothers me more than I thought it would

"I don't have that answer yet. Lana hasn't received her notice yet, so I'm waiting for her. If her notice comes in the next day or two, we can use the same movers and take one truck." Bud explained.

"It makes perfect sense to me. We're in the middle of a murder investigation, anyway. I won't bore you with the details until you get here. If we're lucky, we'll solve it by then." We said our goodbyes, and with a tired body and mind, I drove home.

The following day brings bright sunshine and no fog like yesterday as I followed several fishing boats into the boat launch parking lot. Taylor and Tuttle waited in the boat for me. "Good morning, Deputies. You sure made it to the lake early this morning."

"Morning, Sheriff." I hear from both of my guys.

"I pulled Tucker's file. We arrested him several times for drug possession. One of his arrests was almost to the distribution level. Both of you were in on the arrest. Tuttle, you were new to us then, just like you said. I'm impressed you remembered the name. The weird thing is there is no mention of family. A friend bonded him out of jail."

Deputy Taylor's eyebrows met in the middle as he pondered the information. "I remember Tucker now. We got him on the drug charge from a speeding ticket. He drove a motorcycle around 100 MPH on the major highway over by the Snappy Mart. Last I saw him, he was in the grocery store with a blonde-haired girl hanging off his shoulder, but that was a long time ago. I wonder if she is the deceased female."

"That's him. Once we find the girl, we'll begin our investigation with the drug aspect. Was he dealing again? Who is he supplying? I'll let you two visit his employer." I advised while searching the shoreline again. We need to get a head start on this investigation if it involves drugs. With drugs in the picture, more deaths are likely to occur. If Tucker remained in the drug business, he sure kept it under the radar.

The next few hours crept along. Finally, we made our way to the other side of the cove and had just lowered the ropes again when the DNR boat showed. "Hey, Sheriff. Want us in the same area?"

"That sounds good. We should meet in the middle in a few hours. From there, I'm not sure what our plan will be for the afternoon." I listen as Tuttle and Taylor pull on the ropes. The ropes give off an eerie sound sliding against the boat's side with excess water dripping from them as the guy's tug.

"Have you roped something?" Not receiving an answer, I look over the boat side, trying to glimpse their haul, but the hook comes up empty. Turning to the guys, I watch as they throw the hook in the same area. By the looks on their faces, the dropped cargo is a concern. The rope crawls through the water as the guys try to snag the girl.

With several more attempts under their belts, they relinquish the ropes. We park under a shade tree and have a bite of lunch. The DNR vessel continues its search, but they come up empty too. McAlister glides his boat right alongside ours and ties off. His men are the same age as Taylor and Tuttle. They enjoy conversation while McAlister leans my way.

"What do you think about this murder, Sheriff? You have an idea lurking in your brain." McAlister says with a playful grin.

"Well, for starters, a fisherman found a male's body on Monday. The male has an arrest record for drugs. Now, we're looking for a female. That's all I have right now. I can't attest to the connection for the deaths yet. Not until I have the female's identification." I explained. I'm determined not to mention anything further because McAlister is liable to tell the world before my news conference. If McAlister weren't so easy to look at, he would be easier to ignore.

I gave the guys a little extra time for lunch, but when I saw them looking over the edge of the boat, I knew its time. "Ok, guys, it's time to start the drag again. Thanks, McAlister, for your help. We appreciate it."

He waves his hand as he shoves his boat away from ours. Tuttle works the trolling motor with precision. He slowed close to the same area as before. I noticed the waves breaking onshore to the left of where we were. Tuttle points downward and speaks with Taylor before they turn my way.

"Sheriff, we are dropping the rope here. It might be a little close to the bank, but we will drag towards the middle of the cove. The current is breaking on this side today. I think she's in this area."

There was no reason for me not to agree, so I did. I watched the hooks sink in the water, praying for a sign. Seconds turned to minutes and nothing. They repeated the process and felt a tug. When we inspected the hooks, we stared at a glob of blonde hair.

"We have something, McAlister. Blond hair on one of our hooks. Move your boat closer and drag the same area. She's down there." I said with an edge of excitement.

An hour later, Taylor looks at me, "We've got her, Sheriff. Grab a line."

I reached over the side and yanked on the rope as my shoulder screamed in misery. Several seconds later, a dark shape forms in the water. I can't believe we found the girl.

"We have her, McAlister. Taylor and Tuttle are pulling her in now." I look over at him, and he recognizes the weight of the body. Without asking, he boards our boat and works with the guys loading the girl. When they remove the hooks, she slips on the boat deck and lands on Tuttle's shoes. He freezes in place because he's unsure of his next move.

McAlister has been around a while, so he gently lifts the girl's torso from Tuttle's shoes and lays her to the side. "You okay, Tuttle? You look a little squeamish." McAlister touches me on the elbow as he passes me on his way to his boat. A chuckle escapes his mouth on his way.

"Fantastic, guys. Thank you for your efforts. Now we need to get her to the medical examiner's office. Can you call Harold to meet us at the boat ramp to pick up the body, Taylor?"

Tuttle never spoke after the boat incident. He ties off the trolling motor, walks to the steering wheel, starts the boat, and drives us to the boat launch. While we wait for Harold, we cover the girl with a tarp. Two water deaths in three days are too much for anyone.

After Harold arrives, we load the girl into the wagon and watch as Harold takes a left, returning to town. "I'm heading to the office. You two deserve the rest of the day off. See you tomorrow."

Both faces light up with a bit of downtime. They load up and head towards town too. I watch as they pull into the car wash. They refuse to park the boat without washing it. I wouldn't give up either deputy for a million dollars. These two are mighty impressive, and a million wouldn't come close to their worth. I just hope the next person I hire fits in with the rest. All of my deputies are friends, and that makes me feel good.

The Sheriff's Office is busy when I enter the back door. Maggie rushes to my side. "Thank goodness you're here, Sheriff. There is a woman in the lobby refusing to leave. She claims to be Tucker's mom."

"Calm down, Maggie. Let me freshen up, and I'll speak to her."

I walk into my office and take a deep breath because speaking to the parents of a deceased child is the most challenging part of my job. Death notices always make me sad. I remember when deputies came to the house to tell me why dad never made it to supper that night. It's never easy to learn of one's passing.

After a few minutes alone, I called for Maggie and asked her to escort Tucker's mom to my office. Maggie stood just outside my office door and extended her arm to usher the lady inside. She wasn't what I expected. While Tucker wasn't overly broad, he was stocky and could handle himself in a scuffle. I've seen what he can do in a fight. His mother was just the opposite. She is petite with red-rimmed and watery eyes from many hours of crying.

"Hi, I'm Sheriff Steele." I lifted my hand and reached out to meet hers. Except hers never came. I tilted my head, waiting for the tongue lashing.

"Sheriff, why haven't I heard from you about my boy's death?"

"Have a seat, and we'll discuss it." I took a seat and opened Tucker's folder. I reviewed the papers inside while the lady stared at me. Time helps to calm people down. "Tucker's file shows his mother and father as deceased. We had no reason to think otherwise. What did you say your name was?"

"My name is Rita Connelly, Sheriff. I am Tucker's mom. I found out from the TV about his death."

"OK. Rita. When was the last time you spoke with Tucker?" I asked while grabbing a pen in case she gave me valuable information.

"It's been at least ten years since we've spoken. But I'm still his mama. What happened, Sheriff?"

"You haven't spoken to your son for ten years, and you expect me to bend over backward to accommodate your concerns. Rita, we're handling this investigation like any other. Leave me your contact information, and I'll contact you when we have something to report."

"Sheriff, I apologize. I should have told you upfront about our relationship. But it doesn't change the fact I'm Tucker's mother. I have a right to know what happened. I live north of here but can travel anytime. Keep me updated, please." Tears rolled down Rita's face as she stood to leave.

I stared at Rita's back as she left my office, wondering why she would make the trip to my office if she hadn't spoken to her son in ten years. So what happened between the two that kept a mom from her son for ten years?

My mind worked through scenarios on Rita's reason for being here when Bud called. Lana's transfers came in, and the move to Georgia is official. He asked me to visit him in Louisiana, so I could help him pack. I explained my murder investigation, and he understood, but I heard his voice crack. Sometimes, our jobs take precedence.

Everyone left the office for the day, so I stayed for a while. Clement stared at me every time I sat at my desk, so I picked up right where I left off. The item of interest is a violin. It is an old violin in its original case. I'm not musically inclined, so I don't have a clue about its value. I wonder how Clement knew about all of his stuff. It took me a while to find the violin case on the store's shelf, but I agreed with Clement's description once I did. The violin is old.

Next on the list is a chain saw. It was easy to spot it in the pictures. The blade was longer than the shelf. But as I studied the picture, there appeared to be a void on the same shelf as the saw. This is the first time I've noticed it. Wonder what sat in its place?

After an hour of inventory, I had a hard time holding my eyes open. My head wanted to droop, but I wouldn't give in to fatigue. Two days on the lake and with the manual labor of dragging the ropes, my body ached.

On the drive home, I cruised the downtown streets, just looking around. The city marked the spot where my dad died, and on quiet nights I ride by to look at the marker. I feel he watches over me and guides me in decisions. If dad were here, I would ask him his thoughts on Bud. It's a big decision, and dad always had an answer.

Continuing around the corner, several young people gathered on the street corner. When I pass, they scatter. Once the kids disperse, the streets turn quiet, and so is my house. As I walk down the hallway to my bedroom, thoughts of Bud swirl.

Doc James calls for an early morning meeting at his office. I entered his office shortly after his call because he sounded stressed. "Hey, Doc, it's Sheriff Steele. Are you here?" I walk around the office looking for Doc James. "Where is everyone? Why did he call me then leave?" I mutter to myself. I push the doors open, leading to the exam rooms when I see two feet on the floor behind a table with the toes pointing upward.

Rushing to the other side of the table, I knew it was Doc James. He's worn the same style of shoes for years. "Doc. It's Steele. Can you hear me?" I feel for a pulse. It's steady.

"Dispatch. This is Sheriff Steele. Send EMS to the medical examiner's office. We're in the exam room. It's Doc James, and he's non-responsive." I end the transmission, and immediately Taylor replies he is en route to my location. I smile because Taylor is a protector.

As I try to wake Doc James, he doesn't budge. When EMS arrived, Taylor had a pressure bandage on his head wound, and the bleeding stopped. EMS checked his vitals and gave him all clear. They treated him for low sugar. "Is he a diabetic?" I question an attendant.

"We'll know in a second, Sheriff." He gave Doc James medicine, and within seconds, the doctor was sitting up talking as if nothing had happened.

"Doc James, you scared me to death. What was so urgent you had me running me over here that you didn't eat?" I stared at Doc James with my hands on my hips.

"I have an ID on the female victim, Sheriff. It is Mary Lou Palmer, as in Preacher Palmer."

"Are you sure? Why am I questioning you, Doc? The Preacher's daughter. What in the world are we looking at here? I must tell her parents now, Doc. Anything else on our victim's?"

Chapter 4

"Yes, Sheriff." Doc James continues. "I can confirm a boat propeller caused the damage to the girl's hand and the boy's back. It occurred post-death. I'm ruling the cause of death as murder. Someone killed them with a 9mm handgun, tied them together, and dropped them into the lake. I found no other injuries."

"Thanks, Doc. I'm glad the boat struck them after they were dead. That would have been hard to handle otherwise. I'm glad you're okay, but you need to take a ride with these guys and let the ER doctor examine you."

"Let's go, guys. I feel horrible." Doc James laid his head back on the pillow and closed his eyes.

Taylor glanced my way and pointed out my hand was blood-covered. As I washed my hands, Taylor addressed me, "Bud and Lana are moving to Georgia. That's amazing, isn't it? I can't wait." A smile spread across his face.

He waited for my response because I wasn't sure what to say. "That is something. It came through easier than I thought." I dried my hands more than they required, so I wouldn't have to look at Taylor.

"Sheriff, are you okay? You have a strange expression on your face."

"Yes, Taylor. I'm excited, and it will be nice to have them here. I've had no one do something for me like Bud, and I don't want to screw it up. But, I must admit, I'm nervous."

"You'll be fine, Sheriff. This is the best thing ever. Now, let's drive over to the Preacher's house and deliver bad news."

We walked outside into the bright sunshine, knowing the next stop will be a difficult one. As soon as our cars pulled to the curb, the front door opens wide, and the Preacher watches us walk up to his driveway. He senses we are bringing terrible news. His hands tremble as he shakes our hands. As gently as I can, I tell Mary Lou's parents that she isn't coming home, ever.

They ask a series of questions of how, when, why, and who. I answer how she died. The others will have to wait until we get more information. Then it's our turn. Taylor starts the questions. The interview doesn't produce much helpful information.

We confirmed Mary Lou was dating Tucker Scranton and has been for years. Mary Lou and her folks didn't get along well because of her choices in boyfriends, so they spent little time together. Tucker was wrong for Mary Lou in high school, and she had a run-in with the law because of him. They have had little to do with her since she refused to leave him. Mary Lou's parents kept saying she chose her path in life. Her parents gave us the name Ava Storie. She was Mary Lou's best friend.

Taylor struggles with the lack of information. "Do parents just let their kids go so easily? I realize Mr. Palmer is a preacher, but if my dad were a preacher, he would hold on stronger, not less."

"It sounds strange to me too, Taylor. Every household is different. I've always said no one knows what goes on behind someone's front door unless you live behind it."

"Wow, Sheriff. That's a striking statement. I may borrow it sometime. Should we visit Ava Storie?"

"We have a press conference today at 4:00 pm. I'm releasing the victims' names and asking anyone to come forward if they have information leading to the conviction of the murderer. Is there anything you think I should add? I don't want to give away too much." "The less you say, the better until we get more information. I can stop by Ava's on my way to town if you want to go to the office." Taylor offers.

"I still haven't written the news release yet, so I'll take you up on the offer. Call my cell if you need me." We climb into our cars and go our separate ways.

Halfway to the office, my radio comes to life. "Sheriff Steele."

"Sheriff, Tuttle. Dispatch sent us to the lake again. People were arguing at a campground and got rowdy. By the time we arrived, they had dispersed. I have a brief description of a few of the guys. The caller stated the group appeared to be males between six and eight people."

"Return to the office, Tuttle. We'll discuss it further." Ideas bounce in my brain while I drive to the office. What are the odds people were arguing in the same general area as the murdered victims? Is that where my two people were before their demise?

"Tuttle, Sheriff Steele." I waited for a heartbeat before Tuttle replied.

"This is Tuttle. Come back."

"Tuttle take photos of the campground where the argument took place. See if you notice anything illegal there, like drug paraphernalia. There is a reason for the disagreement and the location. I'll meet you at the office."

"10-4, Sheriff."

My arrival at the office was uneventful. News crews staked out their location in front of the office as they waited for the news conference. I felt terrible for them because the press conference would disappoint them. It will be short in time and information.

As I put the finishing touches on the release, Taylor enters the office. "Sheriff, I spoke with Ava. She gave me two of Tucker's friends. Ava also told me about a fight between Tucker and some guy down at the bar a few weeks back. This unknown guy tried to pick up Mary Lou, and Tucker didn't like it. Tucker laid this boy out, and he threatened Tucker in front of everyone."

"Sounds like a place to start. Do we have his name?" I questioned with my arm hung over the printer, waiting for the page to print.

"Not yet. I stopped by the bar, but the bartender was off. He doesn't come in until seven. I'll stop in later and see if he can give me a name."

I share Tuttle's afternoon experience with Taylor, and he agrees with me that this escapade is no coincidence. The argument was at that location for a reason. I wish we knew the reason. Did something happen at the lake, and the two kids witness it, or are they part of a larger group?

The afternoon was a blur between Taylor, Tuttle, and the news conference. The press release lasted fifteen minutes, and I described the discovery location and the manner of death. I pleaded with the public to offer information. Now, the wait is on for additional information.

With the activity at the lake, someone knows something. No matter how trivial, it might lead to the murderer. I drove home after the news conference while Taylor stopped in at the bar. Tuttle worked on reports when I snuck out the back door.

Taylor called me at nine with the name Rhett Welch. "I've heard that name before, Taylor. Do you know him?"

"I'm like you. The name sounds familiar. I'll run his record in the morning, Sheriff."

I propped up on pillows while I enjoyed a lengthy conversation with Bud. Afterward, I couldn't sleep, so I used the time to work on scenarios for the murders. Unfortunately, too many reasons came to mind but, I jotted them on paper, anyway.

The following day I entered the office to a borage of messages. News people from every corner of the state called, wanting to discuss the bodies. Since my serial murder case, the local news people have acted like we are friends. I try so hard to keep them happy because I might need them one day, and today might be the day. If we can't find a lead on the deaths, I might turn to the media.

As I sat down in my leather chair, I sighed as the phone rang. "Sheriff Steele." I listened to the caller, but when he identified himself as Sheriff Mullins, I froze.

"Did you say you have two bodies tied together and dumped in the lake?" I waited for an answer, and he confirmed. Next, I asked about the bullet holes in the center of the forehead, and he confirmed this. Finally, I ask if he has a female and a male. He also confirms this. I pause before I continue. "Sheriff Mullins, can we meet? We can meet somewhere in between our offices."

Thirty minutes later, and I sat at a corner table in a local restaurant. My hands were sweaty for fear of what I might learn. Four dead bodies in the lake, isn't that strange?

"Sheriff Steele, I'm Sheriff Mullins. It's been a while since we've seen each other. Thanks for taking this time to meet me."

"Likewise, Sheriff Mullins. This situation caused a meeting of the minds. Something is happening on the lake, and I don't like it."

"Have you identified your bodies yet? Someone spotted ours this morning, so we are still waiting on identification. One of my guys heard your news conference, and he told me."

"I'm glad he did. We can get a jump on these. I'll share what we have so far, and then we can talk again once you have ID." For the next forty-five minutes, I share with Mullins our evidence. He recognizes Tucker's name, but not Mary Lou's.

Then Mullins continues, "I have some information to add to our bodies. Our male victim showed signs of torture. Someone crushed his toes, and several fingernails were missing. The girl was intact. We haven't located our victim's vehicle yet. Have you found yours?"

I shake my head side to side while I ponder on the torture aspect. "No, we haven't found Tucker's truck, and Mary Lou's car remains parked in the driveway of their rental home. So, we assume they drove Tucker's truck to the lake. We have no cell phones, either."

Both of us review what information we have, which isn't much. We each have tons of notes from our meeting. "Let me paraphrase what we know. We found two sets of bodies floating in the lake, both sets shot to death and dumped in the lake. However, one of the male victims has missing fingernails and crushed toes. Does that sound right, Sheriff?"

"As bad as I hate to admit it, yes it does. How about we suggest Doc James and Doc Waller collaborate on the bodies? They may find something together." Mullins suggests.

"I like it. I'll talk to Doc James as soon as I leave here. Until you get more information on your bodies, there is nothing left for us. My team is meeting with Tucker's coworkers this afternoon. If I learn anything, I'll call. You do the same."

We parted at our cars. My head swam with ideas. My heart flutters when I think of the reasons for the killings. The identification of the other set of victims will help steer us in the investigation.

Our afternoon will be one interview after another. The first interview is with Tucker's coworker, Bret, who seemed eager to get his interview over. Taylor joins me in the interview room. I have a list of questions waiting for each person. We take turns asking questions and showing photos of the deceased because photos help us make a statement. I've had more confessions using photos than not.

In the end, Bret was a nervous wreck. He didn't provide any help in the investigation. Bret is a delivery driver with Tucker, and they've been friends for a while. Bret moved into the county four years ago for the job. He and Tucker struck up a friendship soon after he took the job. He has had no signs that

Tucker involves himself with anything illegal. Tucker works and spends time with Mary Lou. However, Bret admitted to seeing Tucker and Mary Lou at the bar when the fight broke out. He described the unknown guy. Bret mentioned Rhett's name, but he's unsure if that is the guy's name or someone else in the bar.

Sitting across from Bret, Taylor glances my way as I write a note about Rhett. We let Bret leave with the promise he wouldn't travel out of the county without our knowledge. Next on the list is Roland. Taylor escorted him into the interview room. He had sweat beaded on his upper lip before he walked into the door.

"Roland, I'm Sheriff Steele, and this is Deputy Taylor. We have a few questions about Tucker Scranton." I watched as he shook his head. He couldn't even bear to give me an answer.

Taylor started the interview, and I ended it. Roland and Tucker attended high school together, and Tucker helped him get a job. Roland has never seen Tucker do drugs or sell them. He said Tucker and Mary Lou planned to marry, but Mary Lou was in nursing college. Last Tucker said, his parents retired in Florida. When Taylor asked Roland about the lake, he offered some insight by telling us Tucker and Mary Lou camp at the lake when they get a chance. If they don't have time to camp, they enjoy picnics. They have little money because of the college bills, so they spend time at the lake.

Roland had calmed by the end of the interview, and on his way out, he stopped. "Please find whoever did this to Tucker and Mary Lou. They didn't deserve to die like this." He shook both of our hands before exiting the building.

Taylor and I took a break before the next round of interviews. Our upcoming visitors can be volatile, so Tuttle is helping us. I slip into my office for a quick second of alone time. I'm not looking forward to the two remaining interviews with Rafael Hernandez and JoJo Gomez. It will interest me to see if they show. They are both in the drug business. With back-to-back appointments, they'll see each other passing, which should lead to an exciting exchange between the two.

Rafael is the first to arrive. Of the two, this is the one I least expected to show. I introduced myself again to Rafael and offered him bottled water, and he declined. Unfortunately, he doesn't appear to be in a friendly mood today as he sits with his back straight and his hands on the table.

Taylor starts by asking Rafael to state his name and address, then he tells Rafael that he is not under arrest, but we would like his help. Taylor continues describing the bodies found in the lake. Rafael fidgets as Taylor lays photos of the deceased bodies on the table. Then it's my turn.

"Rafael, we know you deal drugs and have for a long time. We're not interested in you unless you helped kill these kids. Did you have a drug deal go bad on you? Did the kids not pay properly for the drugs? What happened, Rafael?"

He stews for a minute before he answers. In a quiet but intense tone, his eyes turn dark as I watch them become slits. He says, "I didn't kill those two people. Tucker and I go way back, but he stopped selling dope years ago. He blamed it on Mary Lou. As far as I'm aware, he's straight as an arrow now. I would have no reason to kill them." Rafael turned his eyes down as a sign of truth. I pondered his answer. If Tucker was clean, why is he dead? Before he left, he gave us an alibi for Friday night. We'll confirm it before we mark him off the list.

Minutes after Rafael swaggered out the door, JoJo strolls into the room. I wanted to reach up and knock his backward cap off his head. That is no way to wear a cap, and JoJo starts on the wrong foot. He is the opposite of Rafael. JoJo slumps in the chair and tries to act like he isn't nervous.

I take the lead on this one. He has my hackles up already, and we haven't even started. JoJo asks questions, and we stare at him, not giving him the benefit of an answer.

"JoJo, we have questions about the two bodies found in the lake. The killer used a 9mm handgun to shoot them in the head before tossing them in the lake. You own a 9mm, don't you, JoJo?" I leaned back in the chair and studied his face. His eyes roved back and forth from me to Taylor.

"Hey, lady. I didn't kill anybody." He pushes away from the table and acts mad.

"You can call me Sheriff Steele. We know you're dealing drugs, and you own a 9mm. Can you tell us where you were on Friday night?" His eyes turn up as he remembers that far back.

"I was sick at home. Alone, before you ask." He puffs his chest outward like we will drop the questions just because he answered.

"So, there is no one to corroborate your story, JoJo. That's not good." I placed the photos of the deceased on the table in front of JoJo. He glanced at each one.

"I didn't do that, and I don't know who told you I did, but I didn't because I was sick at home. Ask my girlfriend. She asked me to go to a party at the lake, and I didn't want to go with her friends. She invited some new chicks, and I wasn't in the mood. So, I faked sickness."

Taylor jumps in, "What kind of party and where on the lake?"

JoJo shrugs his shoulders, "I can't answer what kind of party, and it was in a campground. I can have her call you, and you can ask her yourself." JoJo pleads.

"Give me her name and number. That way, I can contact her for an appointment." I said to JoJo. I was feeling neither one of my druggies killed the two people. "Write it down on this paper for me." He handed me the paper with Angela Diaz printed on it along with a cellphone number.

We let him leave too. Neither one of these guys has information about the deaths. That puts us back to square one. We have nothing. As I stood from the table, Maggie stuck her head inside and looked at me, "Sheriff Mullins is holding for you, Sheriff. He says it is important."

I nodded and walked to my office. If he has bad news, I want to be sitting. "Sheriff Mullins. How can I help you?"

"Hi Jada, we have identification on our two victims."

Chapter 5

"Who are they, Sheriff?" I didn't want to give him the pleasure of acknowledging the use of my first name. If we'd been in person, that would have embarrassed me.

"Jose Mendez and Margarite Ramos. Both show their address for your county. Do you recognize the names?" I heard him rustle papers on his desk while I thought about the names.

"No, the names mean nothing to me. I'll run their records and speak with family and friends. Thanks for the information." I moved the phone from my ear to hang up when I heard Mullins still talking.

"Not so fast, Sheriff. We need to work together on this. We each have two bodies. Shouldn't we team up on the investigation?" I'm not sure I want them meddling in my investigation, but we could use the help.

"Allow me some time. I want to run these names by Taylor and Tuttle. I'll get back with you, Sheriff." As I hung up before he responded, I called for my deputies.

"Guys, the other two bodies are Jose Mendez and Margarite Ramos. Both live in our county. They share an apartment. Does either of those names sound familiar?"

Neither guy knows the victims. "Pull the records for both. Let's see what we're facing. I'll call JoJo's girlfriend, Angela, and see what she can tell me." While the guys are out of the office, I review Clement's inventory. I'm between one-half and three-quarters complete. I have to admit I'm proud of my accomplishments. However, it hasn't helped me solve the crime yet.

As I dial the phone, I jot notes on my pad. Angela answers on the second ring, almost like she was expecting a call. "Hi Angela, this is Sheriff Steele. I need to ask a few questions about last Friday night. Can you tell me where JoJo was on Friday night?" I didn't give her a chance to say no to my questions.

I paused, waiting for an answer. She has a soft voice, so I asked her to speak up so I could hear her reply. Just as she was to answer, Taylor entered the room, and I placed her on speakerphone. "JoJo claimed to be sick. He said he stayed home while I went to a party at the lake. It was a few friends from high school, plus a few new ones, and since we hadn't seen each other in a while, we met there. We sat outside around a fire, talked, and had a few beers."

"Okay. Angela. Did anything happen at the party, such as another group try to take over or drug sales?"

"No. Sheriff. It was quite a night. But towards the end of the night, two guys argued about something. I didn't recognize the guys, and I couldn't hear the argument since they were distant from my group. The argument was quick. As soon as it was over, they left together as nothing happened."

"Could any of your friends ID the two guys? I'd like a word with them." Wonder what the argument was about, and could they be behind the deaths?

"Sheriff, I'm unsure. No one mentioned it after they left. I can ask around for you." Angela offered.

"Thanks, Angela. We appreciate your help. Just call the Sheriff's Office when you get their information." I ended the call with not much more information than when I started, but I would like to talk to the two guys.

Taylor stated, "Angela confirmed JoJo's story, but we found out about a lake party. Can Doc James tell us what time the bodies hit the water? If we knew that, we'd know if the deaths occurred while the party was happening."

"Good thinking, Taylor. Let's call Doc now." I leaned over and pressed the speed dial button for Doc James. We waited, and he never answered, so I left a voice mail for him with our question. I didn't consider the time of day. "I need to run something by you and Tuttle. Is he still here?"

"Let me check." He searched for Tuttle in the bullpen when Tuttle rounded the corner. "Come on, Tuttle. Sheriff wants to talk about something."

The guys entered my office and took their seats. They always seem to take the same ones. It's funny how accustomed people become to certain things.

"Sheriff Mullins wants to work the case together since they found two bodies in his county. I want your thoughts. Even though all four victims are from our county, it might be nice to have extra hands." I watched their faces as they processed my request. It didn't take long before they agreed to the extra help.

"Okay. I'll call him in the morning. Did you pull the records for Jose and Margarite?"

Tuttle waved the file in the air. "I have them here." He passes them to me. "Nothing much in there. Both have a record for drugs and speeding tickets. Their driver's licenses show the same address, and both work full-time. Jose is a construction worker, and Margarite works at the front desk at a hotel in Mullins' county. They met in their senior year of high school when Jose moved into the county with his family from south Atlanta when his dad couldn't find work in Atlanta. Margarite grew up here. Her parents are here too."

"We need to handle the death notifications tonight. I don't want them finding out from someone else."

Tuttle was pulling a double shift to cover for the deputy whose wife had a baby boy. Since he's on the clock, he agreed to go with me, giving Taylor a reprieve for the evening. I drove my car in case Tuttle gets called away, and we pull into the driveway of Jose's parents in tandem. His dad sits outside on the front porch and jumps to his feet when he sees our cars.

I walked up first to Mr. Mendez, stated my name, and shook his hand while Tuttle stood off my right shoulder. He reaches around me and shakes Mr. Mendez's hand. I notice Mr. Mendez sweats immediately upon our arrival. He wipes his hands down the front of his lounging pants. "Is your wife here, Mr. Mendez? We would like to speak with both of you."

"Sure. Hold on." He scampers down the hallway and returns, holding hands with a petite lady. Tuttle and I introduced ourselves again, but we didn't extend our hands. Mrs. Mendez had a death grip on a tissue, and we didn't want to intrude. Mr. Mendez asks, "what is this about, Sheriff?"

Standing in the living room, I give them horrible news about Jose. The news no parents should ever hear. Mrs. Mendez crumbled like a rag doll, shaking her head and saying "no" repeatedly. Mr. Mendez tried to compose himself enough to speak, but it didn't last long. Both parents couldn't take the trauma. I placed my card on the coffee table, and we left them huddled together on the sofa, rocking back and forth.

Tuttle didn't speak on the way to the cars. He kept his head down, and I knew his emotions were eating him up inside. Death notifications are difficult to handle, no matter the circumstance, but Tuttle is a softie, and that makes it worse.

We drive to Margarite's parent's home, and the family greets us at the door. Both parents are home along with several siblings, of which Margarite was the middle child. She has an older brother and a younger brother. Once everyone sat, I broke the news about Margarite. As soon as it was out of my mouth, Margarite's older brother, Dante, jumped up and started pacing. "Man, oh, man. I will kill that, Jose. He killed her, didn't he?"

"Hold on. We're just beginning our investigation, and no. He didn't kill her. He's dead too." I explained the circumstances behind the murders to four people whose eyes grew to the size of saucers. They couldn't believe someone would shoot and kill and their beloved Margarite.

"Dante or Arlo, can either of you tell us anything to help in the investigation?" I paused, giving them time to sort the information. Arlo glanced at Dante before Dante answers. Dante is struggling with what to say in front of his parents. "Dante, if you know something, tell us, please."

Several seconds later, "they went to a party at the lake on Friday night. That's the last time I spoke to Margarite. I called her earlier in the day and left a message. She called me back about 10:30 that night and told me she was at the lake. There was loud screaming, and I asked her about it. She said that two guys were yelling at each other. She couldn't see their faces, but one of them sounded like Chandler. I don't recall anyone named Chandler, so I let it go."

Dante sat on the couch and mumbled, "if I had known that would have been my last time talking to her, I would have told her I love her." Tuttle and I watched his face melt into a bucket of tears as Arlo tried to hold them inside.

"Thanks, Dante. If you or Arlo think of anything else, please call." Tuttle and I exited the home and made our way to the cars.

My radio crackled as I opened the door. I called for dispatch, and they replied, "Bud is looking for you, Sheriff. He's in your office." I replied, "10-4," and drove to the office with excitement. It's been a long time since I've seen Bud or Lana, and it will be nice to have them back here.

I entered my office through the back door, and Bud was leaning against the door frame. My breath caught in my throat. I didn't realize how much I had missed him until I saw those eyes. "Bud, how long have you been waiting? Why didn't you call my cell?"

"Slow down, Jada. I've been here for about an hour. I left a message on your cell phone, but dispatch told me you and Tuttle were out making death notifications. Besides, I would've waited all night if it meant I get to hold you."

He opens his arms, and I fall in, waiting on the bear hug. It calms me because this feels so right. "Where is Lana? Didn't she come too?"

"We drove a two-car convoy, and she drove to Taylor's while I came here. The moving truck pulled out this morning, and we hopped in our cars and drove straight here. How about supper? You can tell me what you are working on now." Bud slides his arm around my waist and draws me close. He places a soft kiss on my cheek.

"Let me stick my head in my office and check messages. Then we're off to supper and then home." I said the word 'home' before I thought, but he agreed, seeing Bud's face. It is home now.

I unlocked my door, walked inside, and grabbed the messages off my desk. Bud strolled to the plastic table, holding Clement's evidence, and he glanced at the items. Then he studied the board. "You didn't tell me you were working on this case?" Bud looked at me when he asked, with his eyebrows bunched together.

"I wasn't aware I needed to. This is dad's only unsolved case. I promised myself I would solve it, and it took me this long to open the evidence box." My tone was harsher than required, but I need not tell Bud everything I do and when I do it.

"Jada, I didn't mean it like that. I just thought you would have shared that before you started working on it. You told me about the case last time we were together. I'm glad you pulled it out, and I can help you with it if you want. I've several days before we report to Atlanta. You also need to tell me about your bodies from the lake."

My nerves settled somewhat, and I placed the messages on my desk and turned to leave. "Let's grab supper, then go home. I have a lot to share. I've been a busy girl."

Chapter 6

The following day, Bud followed me to the office. We discussed both cases over a lengthy dinner last night. He agreed the inventory might be why Clement died, and the water deaths will fall to drugs, money, or women. I chuckled at the last statement because I knew he was right. Those three are the top three reasons in any murder investigation.

When we entered the lot, I noticed Taylor and Lana were there. She must have followed him on his way into work too. Lana and I recently found out we are sisters, and I wanted to get to know her, but her relationship with Taylor is new also, so my time will have to wait.

Bud and I walked into my office. I sit at my desk as he rolls a chair over to the corner of the plastic table. His email is already open on his laptop, so I call Sheriff Mullins. "Good morning, Sheriff Mullins. This is Sheriff Steele. I spoke with my guy's last night, and we agree the best course of action is to work together on the murders. I have updates if you have time."

"Can you meet for a late breakfast, Jada? We can get a meal and talk."

"No, I can't meet for breakfast, Sheriff. I'm meeting Doc James this morning. We found out last night that Margarite Ramos works at a hotel in your county. I thought you could check out the hotel and call me with an update on what you find out. We know there was a party on the lake in your county, the best we can tell. Two people got into an argument, then they left together. Margarite's older brother, Dante, spoke to her Friday night while the argument took place. Margarite mentioned the name Chandler. Does that sound familiar to you?"

"Chandler. I don't recognize the name, but I'll ask around and see what turns up. We'll talk later. Thanks, Jada." As I placed the receiver in the cradle, I felt Bud's eyes on me.

"What's wrong, Jada? Something has your troubled." Bud asks with a concerned expression.

"My conversations with Mullins are strange. On two occasions, he's called me Jada instead of Sheriff. Both times we were conducting business. Two people with the same rank should call each other by their titles. That's the polite way of doing things." I stand from my chair in a huff.

"I agree with you. Perhaps I should meet this Mr. Mullins?" Bud asks with an eyebrow lifted and a twinkle in his eye.

"That's it, Bud. I'll call him Gilbert. That should shut him up. Thanks, Bud. I'm going for coffee. Can I bring you a cup?"

"I'll walk with you. We might run into Taylor and Lana."

We enjoyed a fifteen break before Doctor James appeared at the office. He holds a file folder with paper poking out the sides. I introduce Bud to Doctor James, and we go back to my office.

"Sheriff. I have interesting news. Doc Waller and I met. The set of bodies you recovered were the second to die, and the set Mullins found was the first to die." I watched as Doc James laid the pictures on my desk of the bodies. Bud whistled when he glimpsed Jose's toes.

"Let me repeat that, Doc. My set died after Mullins set. So, what does that mean?"

"Nothing other than they might have witnessed the first set die, and therefore they had to die too. The time of death is so close. It's difficult to fathom a reason other than witnessing the murders unless they're all involved in the same situation."

"The only one tortured was Jose Mendez, and someone crushed his toes while he was still alive." Doc James stated as he glanced at the photos. "There was nothing else of significance to any of the other bodies." Doc James left me sitting at my desk with my mouth open. I had no rebuttal.

I walked to the murder board and added the news about the bodies at the time of death. Did I think my two witnessed the murder of the first two? I needed confirmation all four victims knew the others. Were they attending the same party? Or were Tucker and Mary Lou on their typical camping trip?

With Taylor on road patrol, we squeezed in lunch with the four of us. It was nice seeing Lana again as we enjoyed the small talk and nothing about dead bodies or crushed toes.

Dispatch calls for Taylor as we leave the restaurant. So, we wave our goodbyes and head to my car and drive to the office. Lana joins Bud and me in my office. They discuss Clement's case while I whittle on the dead bodies by working on my follow-up list for the case. We need confirmation all four victims knew each other, Tucker's vehicle, Jose or Margarite's vehicle, and we need to find a guy named Chandler. Satisfied with my list, I rolled my chair to Clement's table.

"Do you have any ideas on this case?" I glanced at both with my eyebrows lifted as any idea would be a start.

"I agree with your strategy. If there were no witnesses, the best place to start is the inventory." Lana suggested. Bud asks, "have you found any missing items yet?"

"So far, I've found a missing diamond ring. The ring sounds exquisite, like nothing I've heard before. It wasn't a big box item. I surmise a jeweler designed it for someone special. The price tag might have been too high for this area back when he purchased it. Clement had the ring for years. I can't read the name on the inventory list for the person who pawned it."

Bud and Lana shared a glance. "Can we see it, Jada? We have techniques we use in the field to restore handwriting."

I reached inside the box for the binder holding the inventory list. I found the page with the ring and passed it to Bud. He studied it first, then Lana took her turn. Both agreed. Clement used black ink. Bud suggested we try the UV light test first, and I knew who to call.

"I'll call the crime lab. Doc James has one. If he's busy, Harold can help us." I turned around and pressed the speed dial button. Harold answered, and I explained what I needed. Since Doc James is meeting with Doc Waller again, Harold asked us to come over, and he'd take the picture now.

We jumped in my car and drove to meet Harold. It excited me with the opportunity to find the prior owner of the ring. Harold waited for us at the door, and he led us to a room I'd never seen before. "What room is this? I've never been in here before." I questioned Harold.

"They used this room for storage but not too long ago, we cleaned it out for the crime lab. The more machines and evidence collection we get, we're running out of space. Where's your paper?" Harold holds his hand out, waiting for the paper.

I gently removed the paper from the binder and placed it in Harold's hand. He looked at the area I pointed to, "the one line there is all you need?"

"If you can restore more on the page, that's great, but the one line is imperative."

Harold studies the inventory list and then places the paper in the center of the tabletop. The table lowers almost to the floor so he can stand over it for the picture. He mutters to himself, "this handwriting is familiar." He took photos from different angles with UV light.

"Can I ask who wrote this? The handwriting looks familiar, but I can't place the name." Harold asks, as his eyes narrowed.

"It's Clement Locke's handwriting. I've reopened his case. Bud and Lana reviewed the case this morning, and I mentioned I would like to find out who sold the fancy diamond ring to Clement, but I can't read it."

"Clement, yes, now I remember. I liked him. I didn't realize his case was unsolved. College classes started right after his death, and I never followed up on it. Sheriff, please let me know if there is anything I can do to help. Clement was a fine man. Your dad would be proud."

"Thanks, Harold. I appreciate it. How long before we know if this UV light works?" I pushed because I wanted answers.

"Two hours max. I'll call when the photos are ready." Harold lifted his hand in a small wave as we exited the room.

Once we closed the car doors, Bud added two other techniques to restore the ink if the UV light didn't work. We'd try sulfide of ammonium and hydrochloric acid. Both require a small brush to paint onto the document. The sulfide is less likely to damage the paper, and the acid is just that, acid. I relaxed, knowing I had two other options to restore the ink.

When we turned into the parking lot, Taylor radioed for me, "Sheriff, This is Taylor."

I glanced at Bud and Lana as I answered. "Sheriff Steele, Taylor. What's up?" I prayed for no more bodies.

"We have Tucker's truck. Someone parked it behind the boat storage yard over by the lake. Tucker and Mary Lou's cellphones and clothes are in the truck. We found Mary Lou's purse tucked under the seat with money still in her wallet. So, robbery wasn't the motive. I've notified the crime lab, and Harold will process it this afternoon for us."

"Thanks, Taylor. Is the press aware of the truck?"

"Negative, Sheriff. I'm the only deputy on the scene. The tow truck driver will know, but he won't say a word as he's one of my CI's. The storage lot worker is aware because he called it in, but I didn't give him the owner's name."

"10-4, Taylor." I exited the car with more questions than answers again. Whoever killed Tucker and Mary Lou purposely dumped the truck.

Doctor James was sitting outside my office when I walked inside. "What are you doing here, Doc? I just came from your office." I offered my hand, and he shook it but then used me as leverage to stand. He keeps saying he's losing weight, and I keep waiting to see it.

"I met with Doctor Waller again this morning. He wanted me to see Jose's toes because he couldn't determine what caused the crushing. It first looked as if the toes were under a heavy object, and it fell on the boy's toes, but after closer inspection, someone used a set of locking pliers on this kid."

"Are you saying someone crushed each toe separately? The pain would have been unbearable." My body shivered, thinking about the pain.

"That's what I'm saying. Jose endured extreme amounts of torture before they shot and killed him. I'm uncertain what the killer was after, but I feel sure they got their answer. The killer crushed six of his ten toes. His left big toe gave us what we needed to find the object that caused the damage. The locking pliers fit perfectly into the grooves. If we find the pliers, we can tie the killer to the deed." Doc James looked triumphant while I felt queasy.

Another shiver ran up my spine thinking about someone touching my toes and then locking a toe into a set of pliers. I can't imagine the pain. What information did Jose hold that the killer wanted? Was Jose a drug dealer, or did he owe someone money?

I thanked Doc James for making the trip. This information shed some light on how ruthless the killer is, and I, for one, was looking forward to locking this person in jail.

Maggie came around the corner as Doc James was leaving. "Sheriff, Sheriff Mullins is holding for you. He says it is urgent."

"Always urgent to him. Thanks, Maggie." I walked into my office, sat down, and picked up the phone.

"Sheriff Mullins, what's so urgent?" I say lightheartedly.

Chapter 7

"Sheriff, we've heard chatter from a CI about a hit. Someone is out to shoot someone of status. No one mentioned names yet, but I wanted you to be aware and take precautions. If I need to watch your back for protection, just call me."

"What are you saying? You want to protect me. I'm good on that front, Sheriff. Besides, Bud is here now, and he'll watch my six." I felt my face turn shades of red as I threw Bud's name out.

Bud walked over to the phone, "Put him on speakerphone, or I'm driving over there."

With Bud's tone, I complied. "Sheriff Mullins, you're on speakerphone with FBI agents Bud Dietrich and Lana Ivey." I grimaced as I hit the speakerphone button.

"Why are they there, Jada? Did something happen?" Sheriff Mullins asks.

"Mullins, this is Bud Dietrich, FBI. When you address Sheriff Steele, please use her title. She ranks the same as you. Second, why do you need to protect Sheriff Steele? She has a Sheriff's office full of capable deputies, just like you."

"I just thought we're fighting the same battle here with these murders, and two heads are better than one, but I can see my mistake. I'll update you if more chatter occurs. Bye, Sheriff." He ends the call abruptly.

"What chatter is he referring to, Sheriff?" Bud asks with wrinkles lining his forehead.

"Something about chatter from a CI. Someone wants to take out someone with status. But who knows what that means? Mullins might have used it as a ruse to come here." I rubbed my hands together as I considered the possibilities in case it wasn't a ruse.

Taylor walks into the office, holding two evidence bags. Mary Lou's purse is in one, and two cell phones are in the other. When he sees everyone's faces, he stops in mid-stride, "what's going on? You look troubled."

"It troubles us that locking pliers crushed Jose's toes, and Sheriff Mullins feels the need to protect me from chatter," I stated sarcastically. This case was too much. I've never liked drama, and Mullins seems to enjoy it.

"Whoa, Sheriff. Locking pliers? That sounds a bit harsh. Mullins doesn't think you can protect yourself, or we're not worthy. I'm ready to show him a thing or two." Taylor fumes.

"Calm down, Taylor. He's just trying to be helpful." I rolled my eyes as Bud grimaced.

I walked out the door to check on things in dispatch, then I meandered to the jail division. With nothing happening, I made my way to the coffee bar. That's the first thing I installed when I took over, especially since I'm a coffee addict, and I admit it. There is always fresh coffee, from black to flavored, from hot to cold.

Taylor called out to me as I passed his desk. He dumped the cell phone information. He has something to share. "What did you find?"

"Not much, Sheriff. No calls or texts on either phone from Jose, Margarite, Rafael, or JoJo and no one named Chandler. The only item of significance is a text from Ava to Mary Lou about the party at the lake. Mary Lou responded by telling her she had a date night with Tucker. But she doesn't go into detail about their date, so we're assuming they were at the lake for a date."

"Have we confirmed all four victims know one another?"

"Tuttle is working that angle today. He hit the streets about an hour ago. We'll have our answer by the day's end." Taylor looked over my shoulder, and I turned my head too. Lana strolled his way, so I knew my time was up.

As I walked off, I remembered the truck. "Has Harold called about Tucker's truck?"

"Not yet, Sheriff. I'll follow up." Taylor answered while staring at Lana. I chuckled as I headed back to my office. It's so sweet watching them together.

My phone rang as I entered my office. Bud was on his cell phone, sitting at the plastic table as I trotted by him. "Sheriff Steele," I answered and grabbed a pen. A note-taker at heart, so I always have a pen and paper. I'm not accustomed to taking notes on my cellphone yet. There are some things I have a hard time changing.

Harold called with news on Tucker's truck. He apologized for contacting me. But Taylor didn't answer his phone when he tried him. My skin prickled around my head. So, now Taylor thinks Lana is more important than his job? I breathe deep to calm myself. Once I regain my composure, I realize Harold is speaking. They have fiber from the driver's seat that does not match Tucker or Mary Lou. Tucker had a .22 caliber rifle behind the seat, and we found nothing else of significance. The call ended within minutes.

"Bud, I need to have a word with Taylor. Would you step out for a moment? I'll explain later." As he left the office, I shrugged my shoulders and winked at him.

I called Taylor to my office and asked him to close the door. "Harold called me when you didn't answer your phone. Do I need to explain Lana is not your priority when you're on duty?"

"Sorry, Sheriff. I heard the phone ring. But you're right. Lana got in the way. It won't happen again." Taylor's eyes turned down, and he rubbed his hands together.

"Check on Tuttle and report to me." My tone spurred him into action. I hate when I must reprimand my guys. I love them all, but I can't have their partners creating weak investigations.

As I waited for Bud to return to the office, a text came into my phone. "Swell, Mullins is texting me now," I muttered to myself, not noticing Bud leaned up against the door frame.

"Well, what does it say?" Bud asks with a grin on his face.

"I didn't hear you walk up. He says Rafael is the reason behind the chatter. He's angry at me for bringing him into the Sheriff's Office for an interview after recovering Tucker and Mary Lou. Rafael frequents a bar known for drug deals."

"It sounds like I'm moving in with you at the perfect time. I'll protect you from Rafael and Mullins." Bud said as he whispered into my ear, then he followed it with an "I love you."

After Bud moves to the chair facing my desk, he says, "tell me what you have on Rafael."

I pulled his file from the stack and handed it over. Bud takes his time perusing the information. "This guy is serious. Did he give you anything in your interview?"

"Not a thing. He said he isn't familiar with Tucker or Mary Lou. When we interviewed him, we were unaware of Jose and Margarite." My hairs on my neck stood up, sending a strange sensation. What am I missing? Is Rafael that dangerous?

Bud continued, "Rafael is a suspect in several 'accidents' However, no one could prove anything. Is he a gang leader or a drug dealer?"

"He could be both. Rafael started out trying to make a name for himself when my dad was Sheriff. He's been in the system for a long time. I don't recall him ever trying to hurt a deputy. That would take it to a whole new level for him." I considered the possibilities and didn't like any of them. Would I have to live looking over my shoulder because of this guy?

After I shook off the odd sensation, I said, "Tuttle should be back by now. He's out confirming if our four victims knew one another. If they are, then I need to determine how close they were. If they ran in the same circles, that might help determine what happened."

Tuttle appears in the doorway. "Sheriff, all four victims know each other. No one calls them friends, just acquaintances. They all grew up around each other."

"We need to speak with Ava again and see what she can tell us about the lake party. That's where it all began and where it ended. Sheriff Mullins is visiting Margarite's workplace. Can you and Taylor go to Jose's workplace? Perhaps we can find coworkers willing to talk with us."

"Sounds like a plan, Sheriff. Talk soon." Tuttle turns and leaves the room after a quick nod in Bud's direction.

Ava knows something, but she failed to share it with us, and that makes me angry. I grabbed the phone and punched in Ava's number. She answers on the second ring in a soft, timid tone. I explained why I needed to see her again, and she tried to put me off. Once I convinced her I could charge her with hindering a murder investigation, she agreed to meet. Grabbing my keys, I looked at Bud. "I'll be back soon."

"Are you going by yourself, Jada? If so, I can tag along."

"Yes, I'm going alone. Taylor and Tuttle are off on another meeting. You're welcome to come. We're meeting just down the street at the coffee shop."

"Perfect. I need coffee too. Let's go." Bud takes my elbow and steers me outside. The humidity is almost unbearable today. These late August days are brutal in South Georgia. Things are so dry that one match strikes and everything could go up in flames.

The drive to the coffee shop was quiet. I made plans depending on what we found out after our meetings today. Somehow there is a connection to all four victims. Every murder connects to something, but what is it?

We entered the coffee shop and pointed to the booth against the back wall. Both of us slid in on the same seat. I'm in uniform, and Bud wears khakis with a navy blue polo boasting an embroidered FBI seal on the left pocket area.

Ava was fashionably late, so much so, I was ready to call it when she entered the shop. She stammered when she saw Bud sitting next to me. I waved her over, and she slid into the booth opposite us. After I made introductions, she calmed a tad. Ava was fidgety as she spoke, and she constantly twirled her ring around her finger. She confirmed her knowledge of the lake party. They invited Tucker and Mary Lou, but Mary Lou never goes to parties.

The conversation needed a new topic. "Ava, did you witness a loud argument at the lake?"

"Yes, I heard it, but the two guys were so far away, I couldn't tell you why they argued."

"What about a guy named Chandler? Do you know anyone by that name?"

We watched as Ava paused before answering. "Chandler? I don't believe I do, Sheriff. Have you spoken to Rhett Welsh? Someone said he fought with Tucker at a bar."

"I haven't yet, but he's on our list. That's all I have, Ava. Thanks for meeting me. I might have more questions, so don't leave town without my knowledge."

Ava didn't wait around after my comment. She bolted from the shop as fast as she could. I looked over at Bud, "that was a hasty exit."

"She lied about knowing Chandler. Wondering what else she is lying about to our faces?" Bud asked.

The heat soared as we left the air-conditioned shop for the parking lot. Before we made it to the car, my phone rang. "It's Mullins," I stated while opening the car door at the same time.

I answered, and the sound was so loud, I had a tough time understanding him. "Slow down, Sheriff. I can hardly hear you." I paused as I waited for an explanation of the excitement.

"Hold on. You and Investigator Davis were at Margarite's workplace, and someone shot at you as you left the building. Are you both okay?"

Bud hung onto every word, waiting for me to finish the call. I took a deep breath before continuing. "Someone shot at Mullins and Davis in the hotel parking lot. The bullets missed them, but they struck their vehicle. Margarite's best friend is Maria Jorge. Mullins is tracking her now because she's been a no-show for work since the party. He doesn't know where she lives, and if she lives here, then he'll call me."

I stared out the window while processing what I had learned. "Was the hit for Mullins, instead of me? Or am I the next target?"

"Jada, I think both of you are targets. Although, I'm not sure they want to kill you, just scare you."

"They'll have to put a bullet in me to get me to stop searching for answers." I started the car, pulled out onto the highway, and headed to the office. Bud didn't speak on the trip to the office. When I glimpsed his way, his eyes were mere slits behind his shades.

I entered my office, and not long after, Taylor and Tuttle arrived. "We didn't learn too much from Jose's worksite. His friend, Raul Diaz, didn't show up for work on Monday. His girlfriend is Maria Jorge. We'll look for her this afternoon."

"Don't bother looking for Maria. Sheriff Mullins is on it. She works with Margarite at the hotel. Now, go back to the part about Raul Diaz. Where have I heard Diaz before?"

Tuttle thumbs a few pages in his notebook. "Angela Diaz, Sheriff. She is JoJo's girlfriend."

"What are the odds? Raul Diaz is friends with Jose while Angela Diaz, Raul's sister, dates JoJo. That's a little close for comfort in my book." I rubbed my temples as I looked for a connection, but this was confusing.

Taylor asked, "Do you think Raul and Maria are dead too, or in hiding?"

Unsure of my answer, I shrugged my shoulders. Did I think Raul and Maria are floaters too? I had no reason to believe they are, yet.

"We'll keep moving forward until something makes us think otherwise. I'll update you when Mullins calls me about Maria Jorge."

The guys left, and I straightened my desk for lack of anything better. I needed a minute to myself. Rhett Welsh returned to my mind, and I typed in his name and requested his arrest record. His record appeared quickly since there wasn't much to it. His address is County Line Road. This unique road has one side in my county, and the other side is in Mullins County. Rhett works on a harvesting crew in the fall for a few months. Then he moves over to construction. Speeding tickets are the only blemish on his record. I wondered if Rhett was a scapegoat. Ava gave him up fast, almost as quickly as she lied about Chandler.

My cell phone beeped in my pocket, so I dug it out, hoping for an update. Why does Mullins text me to call him? Is he worried about Bud? Mullins's voicemail answered. Wonder why he texted me to call if he is unavailable?

Coffee sounded good, so I walked over to the coffee bar. Just as I was pushing the button for my unique blend, Mullins calls. I considered if I should answer, but in the end, I did. Mullins rambled about how Maria and Raul vanished. Since Friday at the party, no one has seen them, and neither Maria nor Raul showed for work. Investigator Davis stopped at their place, a duplex in town. Only one vehicle sits on the parking pad. They pulled the curtains tight so that we couldn't see anything inside. Davis knocked on the door of their place and then the neighbors. No one answered, so he left his card on both doors.

Then I asked Mullins the same question Taylor asked me, "do you think they are floaters too, or did they run?"

When I didn't get a reply, I checked on him, "Mullins, are you still there?"

"Yeah, I'm here. This is the most confusing case I've had in a while. The victims knew each other, and I just don't see the connection. Maria and Raul have given us no reason to believe they are floaters. None of their belongings have turned up at the lake."

"At least we agree. I don't see them as floaters, either. Rhett Welsh is the guy Tucker fought with at the bar. His record is of no consequence. Ava gave him up for a reason. I'm just uncertain what it is yet."

The call ended with no fresh leads. Bud walks over and rubs my shoulders. "I'm not getting anywhere with this case. Let's go out for supper. I'm hungry." Bud winks at me, and he guides me to the door. Clement stares at me every time I leave the office.

"Come on, Jada. Clement isn't going anywhere, and Harold didn't call today either. We'll check on the photos tomorrow." When we left, we didn't tell Taylor and Lana we were leaving. Lana said she would come by the office today to see me, but that never happened either. A sigh escaped my lips as I slid into the driver's seat. The names involved in the murder case kept running through my mind.

"Bud, do you think Maria and Raul are floaters? They vanished after the lake party."

"Jada, turn your brain off for a few hours, and things will look different for you next time you review your notes. It always happens that way. I learned that little secret a long time ago." His thumb rubbed circles on the top of my right hand. I glimpsed my hand in his, and my body gave way to peace. My shoulders relaxed, and the tension ran away.

Dinner with just us was incredible. We laughed about our childhood stories and some law enforcement calls. When we left the restaurant for home, I had a renewed sense. Sleep came easy that night, and that is something that doesn't happen often.

My cell phone rang at 2:00 am, and my dad always said nothing good happened in the middle of the night. A phone call ruined the best night of sleep in forever. I answered it and listened to a dispatcher explain about the drive-by shooting. When they told me the name of the bar, I sat up in bed. It's the same bar where the fight took place.

Bud followed me out the door ten minutes later. "Bud, you need not come with me. Get some sleep. I'll be back soon."

"No way am I staying here. I couldn't sleep until you returned, anyway." He tickled me in the ribs as we parted at the car.

With lights and sirens, we pulled up beside the ambulance. The EMS attendants lifted a guy onto their gurney as I walked over. The guy took a bullet to the thigh area. "I'm Sheriff Steele. What's your name?"

The guy was in pain. He flinched and fidgeted every time the EMS attendant touched him. "I'm Rhett Welsh."

Chapter 8

My eyes grew enormous as I glanced at Bud. "Rhett Welsh. Are you the guy that fought with Tucker over Mary Lou?" It had to be luck because I don't believe in coincidences.

"Yes, but that was before I knew they were a couple. This was different. I was walking to my truck when a fancy older Trans Am passes the bar, slows, and shoots me. I couldn't see the driver. It's too dark. Find out who shot me, Sheriff. They need to pay for what they did."

The EMS attendant motioned they were leaving, and I could finish the questions at the hospital. As they left the lot, Tuttle strolled over to my location. "Tuttle, were you aware Rhett Welsh was the shooting victim?"

"I just heard that. I found the spent cartridge. The crime lab can dust it for us. Maybe we can get lucky with a print." He lifted it in the air for us to examine.

"Do you know anyone who drives an older Trans Am? Rhett described the car as fancy."

"No, Sheriff. But with the direction of travel, they would be in Mullins' county in less than a mile. That doesn't mean they live in his county, but there's a chance he's seen the vehicle." Tuttle suggested. I nodded in understanding.

"Were there any witnesses to the shooting?" I turned my head around the lot as I asked.

"No one claimed to be a witness. At least no one has come forward. Rhett doesn't remember anyone being in the lot with him. He said he left alone." Tuttle read from his notes as he wiped the sweat from his forehead.

It was hot too, and it was the middle of the night. The heat doesn't bode well for tomorrow because it feels tropical, and that brings thunderstorms. We'll be glad to get the rain, but the storms can stay away.

"I'm going to the hospital to see if Rhett has any more information. I'll reach out in the morning." Bud walked over as I turned to leave.

"The Trans Am shouldn't be too hard to find since it's very distinctive. The driver was stupid for using a car like that in a crime." Bud shook his head as he thought about the driver.

A glance at Bud and I stammered. "You like this small town crime spree, don't you?"

He nodded, "I do, and I can see why you like it here." Bud took my hand in his and led me to the car.

Our time at the hospital was useless. Rhett offered nothing else to help in the investigation. He referred to the Trans Am on multiple occasions. I asked him to stand down and let us do our job. Bud questioned Rhett about his involvement in the murders. He admitted to knowing the four victims, but that's all. Rhett said rumors are Jose had problems with a few folks around town. He refused to elaborate on the issues, or he didn't know. Rhett reached over to the morphine drip, pushed the button, looked at us, and mumbled, "good night."

We left his room with still more questions. My tired body needed to rest. Who did Jose have problems with, and what were the issues? Did he borrow money from someone? We never turned on the lights when we got home. We walked straight to bed.

Ten minutes later, my phone rang. This time I sat up in bed before answering it. "Mullins, why are you calling me at 4:00 am?"

Mullins said he heard about the drive-by shooting. He inquired about Rhett's condition, and then what he said had me sitting up straighter. "You're familiar with the car from the drive-by shooting. That's great, Mullins. Let me know what you find out from speaking with the owner. Talk later." I laid the phone down on the nightstand, but there was no way I was going back to sleep. Blood pumped hard in my veins because I went from the shooting to the car owner in less than two hours.

I threw the bedcovers off and walked into the kitchen. As I leaned on the counter, a set of hands reached around my middle and drew me in for a hug. "Why did Mullins call you in the middle of the night?" Bud's tone was one I hadn't heard before now, and I wasn't sure I liked it. Is he questioning my conversations now or jealous of the caller? I work with men all day. If he can't accept that, we won't survive.

"Someone told him about the drive-by shooting, and he recognized the Trans Am. Mullins agreed to locate the owner and question him." Once I answered, I watched Bud's face relax. Then I asked, "are you questioning my devotion to you because I speak with other men?"

Bud paused before he answered. "I don't question you at all. It's Mullins. He seems pushy, that's all."

"I work with men all day, every day. If you get jealous every time I speak with a man, we might have a problem. I'm yours, but you have to trust me. Or you can quit the FBI and come to work at the Sheriff's Office. However, I'm not sure how you would enjoy working for me as your boss." I poked him in the ribs to get a smile because he needed to lighten up.

Bud cracked a smile, but he tried to hold it back. "I'll admit having a Sheriff for a girlfriend varies from anything I've ever imagined. Give me some time to get accustomed to it. I'm not letting you go. I can promise you that." Bud grinned at me.

I was at the office early for a change. Bud was still sleeping when I left. I didn't have the heart to wake him. The smile on his face was too pleasant to disturb. My crew stacked reports from the last few days in my inbox. One by one, I sorted through them. I laid Tuttle's report on the drive-by shooting to the side of my desk. Rhett Welsh needs another interview. He knows something. I just don't know how much.

Bud called at nine, upset that I had left him. I reminded him he needed the sleep. Otherwise, he wouldn't have slept until nine. We chuckled, and he promised to see me soon. With time to spare, I picked up the inventory list. As my eyes shifted down the page, I startled myself by remembering the UV photos. I snagged the phone and dialed Harold. He said he thought I had forgotten him.

Five minutes later, I stood in front of Harold. "Where are the photos? I can't wait to see them." Harold handed me several photos and grinned.

"These photos will please you. The name of the seller is legible." Harold beamed.

"Harold, I cannot thank you enough for this. You're amazing." I scooped up my photos and ran out of the door. Excitement coursed through my veins as I couldn't reach my vehicle quickly enough.

In my hands held valuable information on Clement's case. Who sold the ring to Clement, and why? I sucked in my breath as I slid the photos out of the envelope. The photos turned the list into a masterpiece with UV light. With the names legible, I considered having the inventory list photographed in UV light. The images would preserve the list if we needed it again.

I ran my finger over the seller's name. Alton Hollis sold the ring. The name Alton sounds familiar, but I can't put a face to his name. Harold didn't mention it if he remembers Alton. Since I don't know Alton directly, I'll run his record when I get to the office.

Although, if he owned a ring of this value, he should be arrest-free.

The office was quiet on my arrival, so I let myself in through the back door. I needed alone time, but Bud sat at the plastic table, working on his emails. I cringed inwardly because I wouldn't have any quiet time. My desk chair creaked as I sat down. Bud didn't turn around to face me as I walked by. "Everything okay, Bud?"

"Not really. Lana and I received notices we are working on the Presidential visit to Atlanta. We leave in two hours." Bud looked at me with a sadness I hadn't seen from him before.

"How long will you be away?"

"At least three days. One to prepare, the visitation day, and then our cleanup day. I won't be far, though." Bud stepped over to my desk and pulled me up into his arms. We hugged for a minute, and it felt right. "I'm going back home to pack. Then I'll pick Lana up at Taylor's. I'll text you when we arrive in Atlanta." Bud rubbed his hand down my arm, took his laptop, and exited the office.

Now, my mood is somber. I felt terrible about wanting quiet time, and I wasn't looking for Bud and Lana to leave, just a little space. I sat at my desk and entered the name Alton Hollis into my computer. In seconds, Alton's background appears. He owned a vast farm on the outskirts of town. The home was one to remember. It was two stories with enormous columns on the porch and a circular drive out front. To reach the main house, you must pass through black iron gates with a sign on them. 'You are entering Hollis Farms.' How could I forget this place?

Alton's background listed him as deceased. He died four years ago, which was years after he sold the ring to Clement. His wife died of cancer ten years ago, and I bet he used the money to save his farm. The farm spent months in foreclosure before Alton settled it. Alton had a heart attack in the pasture behind his house. After reading this story, I checked the tax assessors' records, and Alton's farm has been sold three times since his death. Should I assume Alton never had children? Dad always said, never assume. Next, I pulled county death records for the last name Hollis. Only Alton and his wife showed. Then, I searched the internet for deaths with the surname of Hollis. Bingo! The Hollis' had a son, but he died in the service. The entire family is dead.

Where does that leave me? Without a lead is where it leaves me, but I needed the information, anyway. Now, I'll determine who stole the ring. The media might help if I can't find another way to locate the ring, even though I'm not a big media fan.

With my cell phone blaring, I plucked it from my pants pocket. I answer before it switches to voice mail. Mullins calls. He wants to meet for supper, and he suggests I bring Bud. "Sheriff, Bud is on his way to Atlanta for the President's visit. Where do you want to meet?"

Forty-five minutes later, I parked beside a cruiser at the front door of the best diner in a hundred-mile radius. Their onion rings were like no other. Mullins took the booth in the back, and he sat with his back to the wall. He grinned and waved when I entered.

"Sheriff," I stated as I slid into my side of the booth.

"Sheriff Steele. Thank you for coming."

When I looked at him, he wore a lopsided grin on his face. "Why the smirk, Sheriff? Did I miss anything?"

"No. I couldn't believe you agreed to meet me, and I didn't have to beg. We're getting somewhere now, aren't we, Jada?"

My neck turned red, and then my face turned red. Before I blew a gasket, Mullins placed his hand over mine and told me to calm down. "Sheriff, I understand you're with Bud. But, if there's any chance with you and me, would you give me the word?"

Mullins caught me off guard, and I was speechless. Nothing came out of my mouth, which was good since I would have said things I would have to apologize for later. I took my hand from his and stared at him. "Have you lost your mind? I'm here on business. Nothing more, nothing less. Let's finish this so I can be on my way."

With his chest puffed out, Mullins pulled his notebook from the bench. He stated the Trans Am car owner is Juan Roberto. Investigator Davis spoke with Juan, and Juan let his cousin, Mateo Colon, drive the car. Juan hasn't a clue what his cousin did while he had the car in his possession. His gunshot residue test was negative. Juan is locating his cousin and will call David with his information.

I enjoyed dinner even though Mullins pouted. Once I finished eating, I escaped his company and drove back to the office. Since Bud is away, I can work on Clement's case at night. During the evening, I cleared several more lists. So far, the ring is the only missing item. Did Clement die because of a stupid diamond ring?

Reports and messages covered my desk when I arrived at the office the next day. I was just here, and I wondered when someone placed them on my desk. They were not there when I left last night. The most critical files sit on top, making it easier for me. Maggie must be in the office because she keeps me organized.

It didn't take long to initial and sign a few files. Once I handled those, I moved on to the murder file. I dissected the file with available information versus missing information. Cellphones belonging to Jose and Margarite are missing. We haven't searched their apartment, and Jose's vehicle hasn't been located yet.

Maggie walked into my office with a strained expression. "Sheriff. Can I have a word?"

"Sure. Take a seat." Maggie shuts the door as she makes her way to her favorite chair.

I cringe because anytime Maggie shuts the door, the news is never good. Since I'm trying not to multitask in front of people, I lay my pen down and flip my phone over on its face.

"I didn't want to say anything, but we need help on patrol. With Trevor out for the baby, we haven't had a full staff. We exhaust Taylor and Tuttle because they're pulling extra duty. Have you heard anything about our chance to hire someone?"

Maggie took a leadership role at the office. It impressed me. She's not one to step up and offer suggestions. Her primary goal is to keep me organized and be my gatekeeper. "Why haven't I noticed this? No one has mentioned anything to me about being short-staffed."

"The guys didn't want to burden you since you are working Clement's case and now the murders."

"That's not an excuse. It's my choice to work on Clement's case when we had nothing else. I admit I'm disappointed in the murder case outcome, but now, I understand. Thanks, Maggie, for bringing it to my attention. I'll speak with the guys and check on the new hire with the city council."

Maggie exited the office, and I felt like I had let down my troops. Not only did I not check on them, but I also spent hours on Clement's case last night when I could have worked on the murders. I committed to myself that I would work on the murders until we had solid leads. Then I could shift to Clement.

With my list in hand, I checked on the BOLO for Jose's vehicle. There's no activity on it. I discussed the search warrant for Jose and Margarite's home with Taylor and Tuttle. They wanted to be on the search team. We agreed 11:00 am would be an excellent time to meet. I updated the guys on Jose's vehicle.

"Could one of you ride over to the boat ramp and check the storage yard for Jose's vehicle? If the murders occurred at the lake, his truck must be nearby." I jotted a note next to Jose's truck as a reminder.

Taylor piped up first, "I'll check the storage yard right after the search warrant."

"See you both soon. I've got two calls to make, and then I'll meet you at Jose's."

Mullins called my cellphone as the guys left my office. I answered and waited for his reply. When we separated last night, he wasn't in the greatest mood. He needed to open the conversation. "Sheriff, we haven't located Juan's cousin, Mateo Colon, yet. Maria Jorge hasn't shown her face either."

"Are you thinking these people are in hiding? If they are, they must know the killer."

Mullins stammered as he spoke, "I'm not sure what to think. Drugs seem to be the logical answer, but that doesn't make it the right one. Have you searched Jose and Margarite's place yet?"

"We're executing the warrant at 11:00 am today. I'll call with an update. I've heard nothing else on Rafael. Have you?"

"Nothing as of late. I can only hope the chatter meant nothing, but with Rafael, you're never really sure." Mullins cut off the call, and I stared at the phone, wondering if he'd call back. When he didn't, I left the office.

Taylor and Tuttle were parking alongside the road in front of Jose's place when I arrived. Margarite's vehicle remains untouched on the parking pad. The house is dark with the curtains pulled tight, and their mail flowed from the box to the ground. Are Jose and Margarite dead, or are they on the run?

We gathered at the back of Tuttle's car before we entered the house. Taylor popped the lock on the front door, saving the county damage charges. Once the door opened, the stench was unbearable. We stepped away, trying to catch our breath. Tuttle covered his mouth and walked into the family room and waved us inside. The house is tidy. Everything in its place, but what is that smell? Could it be a dead body?

Chapter 9

Taylor found the smell. Someone left the refrigerator door ajar, and with the electricity turned off, molded food caused the odor. The sink is also full of a half-eaten meal, as no one bothered to wash the dishes or remove the trash. It appears whoever was eating here left in a hurry.

We meandered down the hallway. There are two bedrooms, one used as an office, and the other as a bedroom. My target is the office. Crates line the wall of the room full of paper. "Guys, can you come in here?"

Taylor and Tuttle appear as if joined at the hip. "Why would two people keep all this paper? It looks like receipts of some kind. Doesn't Jose and Margarite have full-time jobs?"

"Margarite works at the hotel, and Jose works constructions. However, from the looks of this, they might have a part-time job." Taylor leans over and removes the top crate from the stack and thumbs the receipts. Someone coded the receipts to cover the transactions. "Sheriff, are these two drug dealers? I can't explain the use of coded receipts if not."

I meddled in another crate, and it contained the same type of receipts. "Have either of you seen anything like this before?" The knot in my stomach grew by the second. I hope we're not disturbing a drug gang. The county isn't prepared for a violent confrontation.

Both guys shake their heads from side to side. I sighed. Where is this murder investigation taking us? I left the office and wandered into the bedroom. The closet is bare, as are the dresser drawers. Jose and Margarite left in a hurry, taking everything, they could grab on the way out the door.

Since the drawers sit empty, there wasn't a lot to filter in the bedroom. I found a few gas receipts but little else. As a deputy, you always check the toilet tank, and this was my lucky day. "I found the stash. They forgot the drugs in the toilet tank." With gloves, I removed the plastic bag from the tank and placed it in an evidence bag. I held it up to show the guys when I saw pills in the bag's bottom. "Not only do we have marijuana, but we have pills. They might be oxy."

"Great find, Sheriff. I've loaded the receipts into our cars. Because of the number, I had to spread them amongst our cars. I found no computer or phone."

"Lock this place, and we'll return to the office. I want to get a closer look at these receipts. We might need Bud or Lana to help crack the code."

We exited the home, and I noticed the neighbor across the street watching us. So I whispered to the guys to watch my back as I spoke with the neighbor.

"How are you, sir? I'm Sheriff Steele. We're looking for information on Jose and Margarite. Have you seen anyone around their house lately?"

I paused, waiting for a reply, when I realized the older man didn't speak English. Taylor strolls over when he sees the staring contest. I explained the issue, and Taylor did his thing. He carried on a conversation with the neighbor, of which I only knew a few words.

Taylor waves at the gentleman as he guides me away. When we reached the cars, he turned and shared with Tuttle and me. "The old man said Jose and Margarite left around 7:00 pm last Friday. He was out walking his dog when they peeled out of the driveway. People were always coming by their house, and now, nothing. No one has been in the driveway since they left."

"It sounds like they were selling drugs from their home. The stash we recovered is too small for distribution charges. We're back to the drug angle. Have either of you spoken to your CIs about Jose or JoJo yet?"

Both guys shook their heads. Taylor added, "I haven't approached my guy because I wanted more information. I think I have enough now."

Tuttle agrees, and he'll contact his CI, too, even though he isn't sure these murders are drug related. Jose and Margarite might have been into drugs, but Tucker and Mary Lou were not. "If someone murdered Jose and Margarite over drugs, why kill Tucker and Mary Lou? It makes little sense to me."

We acknowledged Tuttle's assessment. The pieces to our puzzle still didn't fit. Something is missing. As I drove to the office, I made a mental note to call Mullins and update him on the find at Jose's.

When we arrived at the office, we entered through the back door. It took multiple trips to unload the crates. We stashed them in the corner of my office. I wasn't ready to lock them down as evidence yet. I still needed the code. Taylor and Tuttle headed off to the bullpen when Taylor returned with Dante in tow.

Dante entered my office with a swagger, and I left my gun holstered. Taylor, always the protector, stood at the door. "Hi, Dante. What can I do for you?" I asked in a pleasant but stern voice as I planted my feet shoulder-width apart, with the right slightly in front of the left. I wanted to be ready in case I had to draw my gun.

"Have you found out who killed Margarite yet? It's been days, Sheriff. My mom needs closure." Dante asks, then turns his eyes down. He looks at his hands while he waits for my reply.

"No, we haven't found your sister's killer. We're following up on leads. If you remember any additional information, now would be the time to share." I relaxed my posture since Dante was not a threat. He wants justice for his sister's death.

Dante locked eyes with me, and I witnessed the man change before my eyes. He took two steps closer to my desk. Taylor did too, then he opened his mouth, "Sheriff, we've waited long enough for the arrest. We told Margarite that Jose was no good for her. You have two weeks to find the killer. I promised my mom she would see Margarite's killer before she dies." He leaned over closer, "two weeks, Sheriff, then it is my turn." He turned and stormed out of the office.

"Well, that went well." I looked over at Taylor, as he watched Dante leave the office. "Is he gone yet?"

"Yeah. I saw him exit the front door. That was some visit. He doesn't seem to like Jose, but he didn't tell us why. Wonder why we only have two weeks? Is his mom sick?"

"Both are good questions, Taylor. In time, we'll get our answers. I'm calling Mullins and Bud with updates. Have you spoken to Lana?"

Taylor shook his head no at the same time his cell phone rang. He pulled it from his pocket and then showed me the caller ID. I waved at him as he headed outside to speak with Lana.

Seconds later, Bud called my cell phone. "Bud. Are you and Lana on the same timetable?"

"What, Jada?" Bud asked, not understanding the question.

"Lana just called Taylor's cell phone, and now you call me," I answered with a chuckle.

"Oh, I didn't know she called Taylor. We have a break, and I wanted to catch you before we go on duty again. If the President leaves Atlanta by midafternoon tomorrow, we're heading south. There is no need to hang back here until the following morning."

"I hope he leaves because I need help." Over the next thirty minutes, we discussed our findings at Jose and Margarite's place, starting with the receipts then moving to the drugs. Bud asks questions to understand the receipts better. He suggested I send a few receipts to his email so he could start working on them now. Bud mentioned the FBI uses a program for decoding codes. If he can't solve it, he'll forward it to a buddy for help.

Our call ended, and I felt invigorated with Bud's help. It's about time we moved forward on this case. Now, I called Mullins to give him an update.

The receipts and the drug stash didn't thrill Mullins. He wanted to see a receipt too, so I agreed to send one over email. Dante's visit disturbed Mullins more than anything. Mullins passed the knowledge of Dante and JoJo being friends. "Sheriff, be careful. All the players in this murder know one another. We are the odd ones out here because we don't know how deep this goes yet. If you can travel with someone, do it. I need to run, talk later." I placed the handset in the cradle and stared at the phone. Mullins sounded strange, preoccupied, and worried. Something was off with him, and his voice gave him away. Does he have some information I don't?

Sitting at my desk, someone gasped and said, "no, no." As I rush out my door, I meet Maggie in the hallway. "Sheriff, a call came over the radio. It sounds like someone shot McAlister from a campground. I couldn't tell if it was our county or Mullins' county. Anyway, McAlister is steering his boat to our ramp. An ambulance is on its way too."

My head had a hard time accepting Maggie's statement. She touched my arm, and with unshed tears, I sprinted for the back door. Maggie yelled to my back, "call me when you can."

Who shot McAlister, and why? Was he on the lake alone? I headed for the boat ramp first. If I could see him, I would feel better, and if he's awake, I can ask a few questions. Traffic was horrible throughout the town. I turned on side streets to avoid the traffic lights, but I'm unsure if it saved me time. Before I entered the lot, I listened to the ambulance attendants describe McAlister's injury. My gut clenched when they said the patient was unconscious.

I had to slow the car to make the turn into the boat ramp parking lot. Flashing lights strobed across the lake as I ran to the ambulance. With his face pale, the attendants worked to stabilize his vitals before they moved him. Blood dripped to the asphalt parking lot while they added an IV. One attendant rubbed his balled fist against McAlister's chest. "Sir, can you hear me?" Nothing. Another attendant wrapped his arm with a pressure bandage.

They increased the dosage of whatever drug flowed into his veins and attempted to wake McAlister. Again, the balled fist to the chest. This time McAlister moaned. I walked over and rubbed his arm and whispered in his ear. "Please wake up, McAlister. It's me, Jada. Don't let these scumbags win."

McAlister's eyes twitched several times. Since his vitals were improving, they loaded him into the

98

ambulance. I watched until they turned the corner and drove out of sight. Looking around the lot, I noticed another Sheriff's Office vehicle. I searched for the driver and found Taylor leaning over McAlister's boat.

"Have you found anything, Taylor?" Hopping into the boat, I almost slid down in a puddle of blood. "If McAlister lost this amount of blood, he won't be feeling too good." Blood covers the boat's bottom, circling the driving console. "I wanted to ask him questions about the ambush."

"Look what I found." Pointing to a hole in the boat's side, he continues, "is this a bullet hole, Sheriff?"

Carefully, I tiptoed to Taylor's side, trying to avoid the blood. "It sure looks like it. Use your knife to see if the bullet is still inside." I leaned over the boat to search for an exit hole. "I don't find a hole. The bullet is in the boat."

As I watched Taylor dig the bullet out, my mind wandered back to the campground and the cove. Which cove was McAlister in when the shooting occurred? A commotion caught my attention on the ramp as someone yelled my name. I stood in the boat and scanned the crowd when I spotted McAlister's boss waving at me.

He ambled my way, and we met on the dock. The lieutenant glanced into the boat and grimaced. "That'll be some clean-up job. Did you find the bullet?"

"We found it on the boat's side. Have you spoken to McAlister? He was unconscious when I last saw him." My insides turned mushy at the thought of losing him.

"No, Sheriff. He's in surgery. His prognosis is good, but he has a long road to recovery. He's a healthy guy, so he'll be fine." The lieutenant saw the look on my face and rubbed my forearm as a reassuring gesture. Too bad it didn't help my mood.

We heard footsteps and turned our attention to Taylor. He handed me the slug and stated, "it's a 9MM round. It's the same caliber that killed Tucker and Mary Lou." I dropped the slug into an evidence bag. Whatever is going on out here, it starts at the campgrounds.

"Tomorrow, we're searching the campground. I want to find the casing." I muttered.

The hospital is where I needed to be while I sorted out ideas. Taylor followed me. Since Tuttle has the day off, Taylor is on road patrol and could answer calls from the hospital. My stomach growled as I read the time from the dashboard clock. Food would wait because I need to see McAlister. Memories came flooding back about our short-term romance. It stopped before it took off. We met not long after I started working for dad. McAlister was new to the DNR. We liked each other, but we chose our careers over each other. The circle never made it back around.

Information jumbled my brain as we sat in the surgical waiting room on the third floor. The only pleasant thing about this waiting room is the windows. Two walls of windows allow for sunshine to beam inside. Sunlight always brightens my spirits.

"As soon as I find out McAlister is out of surgery, I'm going to the campground. I want to look around. Unless it's too dark, then, first thing in the morning, I'll be there." Once I made my statement, I answered my phone for Mullins as he spoke of the increasing chatter from Rafael. He rambled on for a few minutes. I stopped him short when I shared about McAlister's shooting. Then Mullins yelled because I didn't call him.

"You need to calm down, Mullins. McAlister is in surgery. Taylor and I are waiting for the doctor. I'll let you know as soon as I can. Do you think this is the big news coming from Rafael's group?"

"I'm not sure, Sheriff. Rafael's group is too smart to share what they're planning. Only that something is in the works."

Once the call ends, I lay my head back on the wall. Rafael's chatter made me nervous, but I wouldn't tell anyone. That is one thing I refuse to give in because no one or nothing will scare me away from doing my job. Was McAlister's shooting planned or happenstance? Did the shooter expect him to be in that cove today, or did McAlister make the guy nervous about being that close?

McAlister's lieutenant joined us in the room. He figured we had no news, so he took a seat and laid his head back too. However, once a few minutes passed, he informed us it surprised him McAlister made it to the hospital with the amount of blood he loss.

My gut constricts, and this time I run for the bathroom. As I lean over the toilet bowl, expressing what little stomach contents I had, I wondered why the lieutenant keeps repeating McAlister's blood loss. Does he know about our courtship, and if he does, that was years ago, who cares? Maybe he's pushing my button because I'm a woman.

Chapter 10

My nauseous stomach concerns me because I'm not one to get sick. I'm not ill. I don't think. However, I'm tired, and that could be the reason I feel nauseous. After returning to the waiting room, I lay my head back on the wall, and before I realize it, Taylor prods me awake. The lights are bright in the waiting room, and everyone stares at me. When I realize where I am, I jump up, wanting to check on McAlister.

"I'm McAlister's surgeon, Dr. Wood. The surgery went well. We'll monitor him for a few days. He remains unconscious, but I suspect he'll wake later this evening. One person can see him now." The doctor looks at me, and I nod my head. I follow him down the hallway without a glance back.

The doctors hooked McAlister to every machine possible. He even has a bag of blood slowly dripping into his veins. He looks so peaceful lying in his hospital bed. I slide a chair over to the side of the bed. My hand rubs his arm as I speak to him. I tell him about the case, and I remind him I need him to survive. He continues to sleep. I lay my head on the side of the bed, and I fall into a dream-filled sleep.

I dream of Clement, the floaters, and of McAlister. We sit along a lake bank and talk. Then, suddenly, bodies pop up onto the surface of the water. We jumped into his boat and recovered bodies because they kept popping to the surface. A nurse bumps my leg and thankfully wakes me from a horrible dream.

"Are you okay, Sheriff?" She asked me with a soft voice.

"Not really. Horrible dreams, a friend hanging on, and a murder I can't solve." When I see her face, "I apologize for laying all of that on you." I run my fingers through my hair.

"Would you like a chair that makes into a bed? I can get one for you or something to drink."

"No, thanks. I'll slip out for a minute, but I'll be back. I'm not leaving this hospital until he wakes." Before I leave him, I rub my hand down his forearm when he mumbles something.

The nurse steps closer to the bed. "You might leave soon Sheriff. It looks like he's waking."

I walked back to his bedside and started talking, asking him to open his eyes. He mumbled, his eyes twitched, he moved around in the bed, and then his eyes opened. I couldn't stop the tears. Maybe it was from relief, and perhaps exhaustion took hold. Whatever it was, they wouldn't stop.

McAlister lifted his arm to wipe my tears, but I wouldn't let him. I held onto his hand while the nurse checked his vitals. He asked for water, and that was the best thing I had heard all day. The nurse produced a Styrofoam cup with ice chips. Her instructions were strict—only a few at a time.

I fed McAlister ice for thirty minutes. Then he started talking. "Thanks for being here, Jada. I'm not sure how you found out about the shooting, but I'm glad you did."

"The radio. Maggie listened to your call over the dispatch radio. I saw you at the boat ramp, but you were unconscious when I arrived. Taylor dug a slug out of your boat. It's the same caliber that killed Tucker and Mary Lou. I hate to ask this, but do you remember anything?"

"I was on water patrol. Same as any other day. I thought I saw a movement at the campground, and I turned into the cove where we found the bodies. The last thing I remembered was someone in a ball cap. They looked male because of the stance, but I couldn't see his face because of the distance. Then, I heard the shot, and I dropped to the floor. I guess I didn't drop soon enough."

"Is this a normal route for you? Do you patrol the same areas every week in the same order?"

"No, our areas change depending on what's happening. Today, I just got lucky. I was on my way back to the boat ramp when it happened." McAlister grimaces as sharp pain courses through his body.

"I'll let you rest, but I'll be back, McAlister. Don't scare me like that again." I rubbed his arm on my way out.

The hospital was quiet, with dimmed hallway lights. I found myself alone in the hospital parking lot in the middle of the night. The realization was startling. I searched my surroundings before climbing into the car. The radio squelched as I closed the door, and I waited for the reply. When one didn't come, I grabbed the radio and asked the dispatcher for a response. "This is Sheriff Steele. Repeat the last transmission."

"Dispatch to Sheriff. Taylor isn't responding to radio calls. In his last report, he had a meeting at midnight with his CI. No name and no location." I tried not to curse, but after today, I couldn't hold it back any longer. Before I left the lot, I pulled my phone out of my pocket. I have ten voicemails from Bud and two texts from Taylor. I breathed a sigh of relief when one message told me his location.

"Dispatch. This is Steele. Taylor is fine. He'll be on the road within thirty." I calmed their anxiety down a notch, but it did nothing for mine. Leaving the lot, I pressed the speed dial for Taylor. When he didn't answer, I sped down the boulevard towards Taylor's meeting place. Just as I turned the corner, I met Taylor exiting the lot. He recognized my car and stopped. "Hey, Sheriff. What are you doing out here?" Taylor casually asked.

"We've been trying to find you. You were away longer than expected, and dispatch got nervous. I had just left the hospital when I got the call on the radio. Did you find out anything?"

"Not much. Rumor has it Tucker is clean. When he and Mary Lou discussed marriage, he agreed to leave that life behind him. Now, Jose and Margarite are drug dealers. The receipts are from drug deals. He can't decode them, but he figures each crate is a runner. That's how they keep track of the sales. My CI also shared that Jose is a gambler, but he's not sure if that helps. He mentioned Margarite put an end to that pastime. There is a guy over in Mullins county with the initials RT. RT and Jose hang together sometimes."

"That's useful information, Taylor. Thanks for meeting your guy. We'll add the information to the murder book tomorrow." We waved at each other as we pulled out of the lot.

As soon as I turned onto the Boulevard, Bud called. He's frantic when I answer. I talked with him on the drive home. He and Lana will be home on Saturday. I explained what happened with McAlister. My voice must have expressed emotion over McAlister because he asked if we were close. That turned into a more extended conversation than I had expected. We were still talking when I made it home. Dropping into bed, I remember nothing until nine the following day.

Even though I'm not expected at eight every morning, I feel better when I show early. This morning is an exception to that rule. I rolled over in bed to a pounding headache and achy muscles. Why am I so sore? I don't remember doing anything strenuous yesterday.

On my second cup of coffee, my mind flies to McAlister. I called the hospital, and the nurse shared he ate breakfast this morning and is sitting up in a chair. Once I hung up, I smiled. There is nothing in this world that will make me happier than to see him leave that hospital. After these years, it's sad something life-changing brings two people back together. But I cringed as I thought back on how close to death he was lying on the gurney as they slid him into the ambulance.

Driving to the office, I changed course and went to the hospital instead. The nurse was correct. McAlister was sitting in a chair watching TV when I entered his room. "Would you look at you? Sitting in a chair, not even twenty-four after being shot."

"Thanks, Jada, for staying with me last night. It was nice to see you when I opened my eyes." He reached for a hug. I complied. It felt good, even though it was a little awkward. We haven't shared a hug in years.

"I was glad those eyes opened after what I witnessed on the boat ramp last night. You scared me, and I didn't like it. I'm headed to the office now. The guys are waiting for me to give them an update on your story. Is there anything else you can remember?"

"The guy in the ball cap. The cap had a logo in the center. If I had to guess, it was a dark-colored cap with a white logo. The logo stood out."

"Don't beat yourself up over this. I'm impressed you remembered what you did. Being shot, losing blood and consciousness, and you still pulled it out. That's amazing." I walked over to McAlister, gave him a quick squeeze, and told him I'd see him later.

Once I exited the hospital, I plucked my phone from my pants pocket and dialed Taylor. He answered on the first ring. "I'm waiting for you at the office, Sheriff. I thought we would scout the campground."

"We are. I'm on my way now. I stopped by to see McAlister before we headed out. See you at the campground in a few." I hung up, slapping myself because I forgot I had mentioned that to Taylor. Somehow, I have to get my brain back on track. Now that McAlister will be okay, I can work on myself.

I called Maggie to let her know where I would be for the rest of the morning. Nothing was pressing at the office. So, my mind turned to Bud. While it made me happy he's moving to Georgia, I'm worried we made the gigantic leap too quickly. Can I make a relationship work? Relationships have not been easy for me. I find myself confused now that McAlister is back in the picture.

Taylor, Tuttle, and Mullins wait for me at the campground, "Sheriff Mullins, why are you here?" I faced Taylor and Tuttle when I asked the question. Taylor shrugged his shoulders.

"I was over at our campground when the deputies showed. I came over and offered my help. Is that a problem?" Mullins lifted an eyebrow while he waited for an answer.

"Not at all. We'll gladly accept help. I want to inspect the ground for the spent shell. If the shooter didn't police his shell, it's still here." I looked around while I stood at the top of the hill leading down to the lake.

Ten steps to the right, and I could see the location of McAlister's shooting. I just couldn't figure the shooter's distance to the water. I reiterated McAlister's description of the shooting to the group, and we fanned out.

With the sun shining, I looked for a shiny object tucked under something or behind a rock. Every so often, I checked my target area because I wanted to stay in the proper proximity. I was a little too far to the left, so I adjusted my search area and glanced down. Drag marks ran from my site towards the lake, with one side more profound than the other.

"Can someone come over here? I found drag marks, and I want to get your take on it. What caused these marks? Could this be shoe marks?" I ran my finger through one mark. The depth was more profound than expected. I don't remember any victim wearing shoes with heels that could cause these.

The guys inspected the marks. No one explained the patterns. Tuttle asked, "does anyone have a tape measure? I want to measure the distance between the marks. It looks like they are further apart to start, then draws closer. I thought it might be a full cooler, but the wheels wouldn't shift so that the distance would remain constant."

Taylor, with his eyebrows bunched together, "I think Tucker wore work boots when we found him. He would be heavy enough to create those marks." He looked at the lake from his vantage point. With his gun in hand, he aimed it towards the lake. I watched him figure the line of sight.

"Here you go, Sheriff. It's the spent shell." Taylor leaned over and scooped the shell into an evidence bag. He handed it to me after he sealed it.

"I'll take this by the crime lab on my way into the office. I'm thinking about surveillance on the campground tonight. What are your thoughts?" I made eye contact with each guy. They need to see I'm serious.

Mullins was the first to speak. "I agree with surveillance, and I'll join in tonight."

I didn't care who took the first shift with me. Time is of the essence, and I have to move. "Thanks, Sheriff Mullins. Let's meet at the boat ramp at seven, and we'll walk to the campground."

"See you then, Sheriff." Mullins turns and walks away.

We walked to our cars in silence with ideas running through my head at warp speed. We have the spent cartridge and drag marks in the same area. Is that evidence to support the murder of Tucker and Mary Lou?

Later in the day, Mullins calls to confirm our meeting tonight because he thought I would change my mind. When I proved I would meet him there, his mood became serious. "Sheriff, I'll meet you in the parking lot. Do not approach the campground without me."

"I hear you, Mullins. Just be on time, and we won't have to worry about that, will we?" I ended the call, not wanting to argue with someone who's watching my six. Now, to share the news with Bud. He'll be angry, but since he's not here, Mullins will partner with me.

On my way home, I stopped by the hospital to check on McAlister. A lady stood by his side, murmuring to him when I entered. I hesitated before entering, but curiosity won the battle, and I wanted to find his visitor's name. Without so much as a sound, I made it halfway into the room before being noticed. "Hey, Sheriff. Any news?" McAlister asked as he shifted in the bed.

"Nothing yet. Tonight is the night for a stakeout. I'll update you tomorrow on what we find." Since he would not introduce me to his friend, I did it myself. "Hi, I'm Sheriff Steele."

"Hi, I'm Lacy McAlister. His sister." She pointed to McAlister.

Lacy surprised me because he never mentioned a sister. Come to think of it. He never mentioned his family. We weren't as close as I thought. Seeing them together, they favored. McAlister is older than Lacy, but not by much. "Do you live around here, Lacy?"

"No, I live in an Atlanta suburb. I work for a marketing firm, and there isn't much of that down here. I'm hoping to start my own firm, and then I can work from anywhere. A few more years, and then I'll be ready." She looks down at her hands before looking at me again. It makes me wonder if everything is okay with McAlister.

"I'll leave you two alone since I have to report to the lake at seven. We'll talk tomorrow. Nice to meet you." After saying my pleasantries, I left the room in search of McAlister's doctor. When I couldn't find him, I stopped the next best thing, his charge nurse.

She commented about not talking to me since I'm not family, but I forced it out of her. McAlister is losing blood from somewhere. They are monitoring it, and he'll have surgery in the morning to repair the damage. She suggested I call around nine in the morning.

With that information, I didn't want to do a stakeout. I wanted to curl up in a chair next to McAlister. My mind won't be on it, but McAlister will be mad if I skip out on the stakeout. He wants to know who shot him, and I can sympathize with him on that because I would too.

I called Bud and listened to him explain why doing a stakeout with Mullins is a bad idea. Then, I had my chance to soften the blow. I won the battle. But I had to agree to take my phone and text him every so often with an update. He says these people are mean. Whoever they are, he reminded me they use pliers to crush toes.

Chapter 11

At seven on Friday night, I step out of my car with my black bag hanging off my shoulder. Sheriff Mullins lifts his eyebrow when he sees it, then he reaches inside his passenger car door and pulls out a matching bag. I didn't comment.

We stand over the trunk of his car and discuss our options. There's slight cropping of shrubs and trees to the north of the campsite. The darkness with the foliage will conceal us as we walk. Both of us wear all black clothing, black ball caps, and we wear a thigh holster. My gun of choice is a 45 caliber, which sits on my thigh. I also have a 38 snub-nosed pistol riding in an ankle holster.

Glancing at Mullins, he wears the same thigh holster and weapon. I feel sure he has a backup, but I'm not asking to see it. He adds extra magazines to his belt. If we need that much extra ammo, we're in trouble. We pull out our binoculars and wear them hanging from our necks. I place a pen and a small pad of paper in my cargo pants pocket.

At ten minutes after seven, we walk towards the trees. We didn't speak to each other. Instead, we pointed out which direction we wanted to travel. The closer we got to the campsite, we let the fire guide our way. People sat around the fire on wooden logs and fold-out chairs. Some were drinking alcohol while others sat and stared at the flame. The scene was a little odd. It wasn't rowdy, and it seemed quiet for a get-together.

We passed within twenty yards of the bathroom. I almost passed out when I walked right into something hard. Mullins ran into the back of me since I was the lead. My bag hit the ground as I tried to recover. We didn't move for a while because it scared me someone might have heard the commotion. When no one bothered to check, we scoped out the reason for the instance. I walked into Jose's truck because someone camouflaged it with tree branches and debris. They knew we had recovered Tucker's truck, so they couldn't take it to the storage yard.

I took my pen and paper out of my pocket and wrote the area to find the truck tomorrow. We covered it again and continued on our walk. A few more yards deeper into the woods, we found a spot to watch the group. I snapped a few pictures with my phone, and Mullins did the same. At eleven that night, a guy wearing a navy or black baseball cap arrives and acts like he is the life of the party. He tries to get the girls to dance, but no one is having any of it.

The guy relents and joins the group around the fire pit. We watch them discuss something. One guy raised his voice, stood up, then the guy in the ball cap pointed towards Jose's truck. Within minutes, everyone calms again. We were unsure whether to stay put or change positions. We couldn't afford for these kids to find us. Who knows what they would do with two local Sheriffs?

With flames reaching into the night air, the group sits quietly around the bonfire. At one point, I heard a girl sniffle as if she were crying. Later, two girls walked away together, never to return. A little past midnight, Mullins and I called it quits. Nothing was happening tonight. We inched our way back to the parking lot, not realizing the depth of the darkness.

Our proximity to the group prevented us room to speak until we cleared the woods. We made it back to our cars and leaned on my trunk. Mullins stated, "the activity around the bonfire is not what I expected."

"I agree. It's like the kids are sad, except for the guy in the ball cap. Did he stop by the bonfire to cheer everyone up or to check on the group? Do you suppose the guy in the ball cap is McAlister's shooter?"

"He could be the shooter. McAlister described the ball cap. If we had been a little closer to the group, we might have seen the logo on the cap. It would have helped with identifying the guy. I couldn't see enough of his face to name him, but something about him seems familiar."

"It's time to head home, Sheriff. I'll have Jose's truck picked up in the morning. Once I get the report, I'll call you with an update. Thanks for sticking around tonight."

"Anytime, Jada. Talk soon."

As soon as he says it, I cringe. I try to hide my emotions. But sometimes, it's impossible. He turns around, "sorry, Sheriff Steele."

My phone vibrated in my pocket, and I plucked it out, knowing it was a message from Bud. I haven't texted him since I bumped into the truck. Once I read it, I called him instead of sending a text. When he answers, a sigh escapes his lips. "Bud, it's me. I'm on my way home from the stakeout." He asked all about it, and I obliged. At least I had a reason to stay awake while I drove.

Jose's truck was on a flatbed by nine the following day. Deputy Taylor met the tow truck at the lake, and he secured two cell phones and a few articles of clothing. Before the tow truck driver pulled away, Taylor asked to see inside the vehicle again. While inside, he took the phone charger still plugged into the car. Both phone batteries lost their charge many days ago.

Taylor notifies me of his find, and he follows the truck to the crime lab. No one was at the campground this morning, so he did more snooping. Discarded food wrappers and beer cans were the only evidence proving a bonfire occurred last night. Before he left the area, he placed two trail cams in inconspicuous spots. These cameras might afford better pictures of the group, especially the ball cap-wearing guy.

The bullpen was active for a Saturday morning. Taylor walks in with his arms full of evidence from Jose's truck. "Sheriff, I charged the cell phones on my way back to the office. Jose didn't use a passcode to open his phone, but Margarite did. It will take a minute to unlock it. I'll report to you as soon as I've had time to inspect the phones. What else do you want me looking for other than contacts, email accounts, and text messages?"

"Nothing else comes to mind right now. Let's see what we gather from this. Thanks, Taylor." I turned around when someone called my name over the intercom. The voice sounded terse and asked me to report to the jail division.

Not taking any chances on the request, I trotted to the jail wing. As soon as I turned the corner, I spotted the blood trail on the floor and the wall. I called for a lockdown, which requires all deputies to report to the jail. Next, I called Tuttle on his cell and requested Rufus' help if I had a jailbreak.

As I approached the intake area, my gun led the way. I peeked around the corner and what I witnessed was gut-wrenching. Without another glance, I ran to Deputy Unley's side. Blood ran freely from his side onto the floor. The shank still protruded from the puncture wound. Unley felt my presence because his eyes opened, and he said, "go get him, Sheriff. And call me an ambulance." Before I ran after the escapee, I found a roll of paper towels and made a giant wad, then I pressed the towels into Unley's side and slid his ballistic down to hold the pile in place.

Just as I stood, Taylor appeared at my back with his gun drawn. "What do we have, Sheriff?"

"One down for sure, Unley is as far as I made it. I'm not sure of the extent. Let's go further inside.

Lieutenant Roy has made no contact yet, and he's on duty today." I rubbed my hands down my pants, smearing Unley's blood on the way down.

We entered the intake area and noticed nothing abnormal. Deputies arrived with lights and sirens. I expected to hear from Tuttle, but nothing yet. Our approach continued, and we met Lieutenant Roy positioned in the hallway with a few of his jailers. "Lieutenant Roy, what is the status?"

He glanced my way and walked over to us. "We had a local guy, Dewayne Curtis, here for DUI and habitual violator. Unley had him in the intake area, readying him to enter the jail when he shanked Unley. Then, Curtis raced down the hallway, unaware it went straight to the jail. As he left Unley's side, he apologized but said he couldn't stay in jail anymore."

"This Curtis guy has been here before, right? If so, do any of the deputies have an address for him?"

Lieutenant Roy nodded his head, "I've dispatched a deputy to his mom's house. He lives with her. Something snapped in Curtis. In the past, he was always a model prisoner."

"Let's find him, then we can ask him. Tuttle is bringing Rufus to the office if we need him. Are we sure he left the grounds?" I looked at Taylor, and he suggested we search for ourselves.

I agreed with Taylor, and we struck off on our own. We've completed many searches together, so this should be an easy one. Since most doors lining the hallway remain locked, there are only a few places to hide. My cell phone rings, and I contemplate letting it go to voice mail, but I needed Tuttle.

"Captain Grayson. Taylor and I are searching now. Unley is in awful shape. The ambulance arrived a few minutes ago. Go to the hospital with him. Call me later."

Taylor spots traces of blood on the door leading into the common outside area. We peeked through the small window in the door and saw no one. Then, with a whisper, Taylor lays out the plan. He goes first, always, then I follow with my left hand on his right shoulder. The door opens at a snail's pace, and Taylor peers around the door. I watch him relax as he walks outside into the yard.

Confused by Taylor's actions, I followed and peeked around Taylor's back. Dewayne Curtis is sitting with his back against the brick wall. When he sees us, he raises his hands. "Sheriff, I can't even get away in an escape. No one told me what happens in a lockdown."

As Taylor pulled his handcuffs from his waistband, Curtis stood and surrendered without incident. Then he asked about Deputy Unley's injury, and neither of us responded.

Lieutenant Roy placed Curtis in solitary until Monday when Captain Grayson returned to duty. Curtis could ponder their conversation all weekend. Captain Grayson can make a man's man squirm with his stare.

With the lockdown lifted, Tuttle returned home. Taylor and I filled out a report, and I called Captain Grayson for an update on Unley. Grayson reported Unley is in surgery to repair a broken blood vessel, but they expect him to make a full recovery. I laid the phone on my desk, and when I looked up, Bud stood in the doorway.

"Bud, you're home." I jumped up and ran over for a hug. He stepped back while gawking at my pants.

"Tell me that isn't yours, Jada." He squeezed a little tighter than expected, and then he looked me in the eye, waiting for an explanation.

"No, it's not mine. We just concluded a jailbreak. A repeat offender decided he didn't want to spend any more time in jail, so he shanked a jail deputy and fled. Unbeknownst to him, the door he exited leads into the common outside area. We found him sitting on the ground with his back against the wall."

After I confirmed the blood wasn't mine, we sat and talked for a few minutes before he asked for an update on the murders. I shared additional information with him, which wasn't much. We discussed several ideas, and he thought adding trail cams at the campgrounds might prove fruitful. Then Bud asked about McAlister.

"I failed to check on him today. After we moved Jose's truck to the crime lab, we had the jailbreak. McAlister is undergoing surgery again today for internal bleeding. His sister seems to think it will be a quick surgery."

I picked my phone up just as my text tone sounded. McAlister's sister is texting with an update. "Surgery went well, and he's in recovery."

"That's a relief," I replied with a heart, and I would stop in later.

Bud asked, "any changes in Clement's case?" He shifted in his chair, and while he did, he looked away from me.

"No changes with his case. I still have the missing ring, but I haven't had time to finish the inventory lists yet. By the sound of it, the diamond ring alone could be a reason for murder."

Taylor sticks his head into my office, "Hey, Bud. Sheriff, I've got something on Margarite's phone. Want to come to see it?"

We walked over to Taylor's desk in the bullpen. He has a desk away from the others since he helps me so often. His desk area allows for multiple tables too. Margarite's calls and text messages are visible on Taylor's computer screen. Taylor updated us on his findings. Margarite and Maria Jorge who dates Raul Diaz, are friends, and the ladies shared coded messages via text. I walked up to the screen, thinking if I got closer, I could decipher the messages. When that didn't work, I backed up and looked at Bud.

"These are like the receipts as they use the same language. Print a few of these. Then we can compare the receipts to the messages. My guess is they were in this business together. If that's true, Jose and

Margarite were the true targets. The other deaths were collateral damage."

Lana looked over and asked, "did Maria and Raul kill Margarite and Jose for the business?"

"Good question, Lana. You gave us another avenue to investigate. Sheriff Mullins is still looking for Maria and Raul. They've been missing since the weekend of the murders."

Once I jotted a reminder, I suggested we leave for the day and enjoy the night together. I invited everyone to my house for a cookout. They agreed, so Bud and I left the office and headed to the grocery store for food. Before I knew it, Bud snagged the copies of the text messages and the receipts from Taylor's printer. I knew he couldn't leave it until tomorrow. However, I would be back in the morning because I couldn't leave my cases alone either.

Chapter 12

Lightning threw streaks of bright light into the house on Sunday morning while thunder rattled the windows. Bud found me at the kitchen table sipping coffee and reviewing the case notes on the murders. "I didn't hear you get up this morning." Bud rubbed my shoulders on his way to the coffeepot.

"How could you with this weather? It's the worst storm we've had in a while. I bet the fire department will be busy with lightning fires, and that makes the Sheriff's Office busy too."

Once Bud had his cup of coffee, he joined me at the table. He helped himself to my notes on the case. "Did you identify the guy in the cap?"

"Not yet. Mullins continues to work on it. He says he doesn't recall the guy's name, but he seemed familiar to him." I spotted the word 'receipts' scribbled on the back of a piece of paper. "Have you worked on the receipts lately? I'm with you on receipts being from drug sales. It's the only plausible reason I can find."

I watched Bud as he swallowed his sip of coffee. "Both the receipts and the coded texts messages are on today's docket. I figured you would go into the office anyway, so I will too."

While Bud read the case files, I slipped out of the room for a shower. Once I dressed, I phoned McAlister's cell. He answered, somewhat groggily.

We chatted for a few minutes, and he mentioned they might release him Monday or Tuesday. His news made my day. As I ended the call, I wanted to ask again about the shooting. I'm hoping he remembers something else about the encounter. Also, I need his eyes on the picture of the guy from the lake. The picture might jog memories. But the questions will wait until he is stronger.

An hour later, Bud and I left the comfort of home for a trip to town. My windshield wipers couldn't keep up with the deluge of water from the clouds. Halfway to the office, my radio crackles. I lifted the mic to my lips when I saw it. My feet slammed on the brakes, and all I managed was to point to the sky.

The tornado danced in the sky above our heads as we watched it travel toward town. My response to dispatch was urgent. "Tell everyone to seek shelter, tornado at the edge of the property."

No response came back to me. I looked at Bud because I didn't know what else to do. "Drive, Jada. Get us to the Sheriff's Office." He pushed a speed dial button on his phone and spoke with someone, guessing Lana or Taylor.

As I pulled into the parking lot, dispatch replied, "all clear." I circled the lot to see for myself, and then I drove toward the tornado touchdown site. When Bud's call ended, I asked, "Are Taylor and Lana safe?"

"Yes, but Taylor can't reach Tuttle on the phone. So they are driving over to his place now. From what I can tell, everyone else is okay and no damage to their residences."

"Thank goodness. Look over there. Is that smoke coming from the back of the restaurant?" With lights and sirens activated, we attempted to enter the lot when a massive tree crashed in front of the car. I gasped and hit the brakes with both feet just in time to avert a collision. We exited the vehicle amongst tree branches and debris.

We walked around in the pouring rain to the back door of the restaurant. By the time we cleared the tree, the fire had raged. One car sat in the lot, so we ran to the front of the building, searching for the occupant. Bud broke the window for us to enter. He walked to the back of the restaurant as I dialed dispatch. Bud yelled something from the end of the building. When I reached him, he held a man's head in his lap. It appeared lightning struck the man on his right shoulder, traveled down his right arm, and exited his right hand. He has severe burns on his body.

Dispatch radioed for the fire department and an ambulance. With the fire burning behind us, we had to move the guy to safety. Bud lifted the guy up off the floor by his shoulders and drug him to the front of the building, hoping the fire didn't spread before help arrived.

The victim moaned as Bud laid him down. His eyes darted back and forth, and he tried to talk. I asked him to keep calm by telling him help was on the way. Then, he gave in to the trauma. As soon as the fire department and ambulance arrived, we left. I wanted to cruise through town and check on the damage.

Taylor called, wanting our location. I shared our experience with him and told him we were in the parking lot. Tuttle met me in the hallway as we arrived. "Hey, Tuttle, is everything okay at your place?"

"Yes, Sheriff. I helped a neighbor find his patio furniture, which blew away in the storm. It looks like the county got lucky today. I hope we're in for better weather now."

"Me too, Tuttle." I entered my office and sat in my chair, laying my head back. This morning had been one for the record books: storms, tornado, a man sustaining a direct hit from a lightning strike. I can't recall another lightning strike victim in our county. He'll be a legend if he survives the injuries because his wife will see to that.

A little while later, Bud and Lana enter my office holding papers. They didn't even ask if I was busy. They just jumped right in with their discovery. "Sheriff, I discussed the receipts and messages with Lana because they're bothering me. The codes looked familiar, but I couldn't figure out why until now."

Lana picks up the story from here. "Bud and I worked a case four years ago in Louisiana involving coded receipts. We came in on the tail end of the investigation, but our tech guru decoded the messages. These receipts looked eerily similar. If you're okay with it, I'd like to send a sampling of the receipts and the text messages to Tony."

"No question about it. Send them. If they look that similar, I wonder if Margarite is part of a larger drug smuggling operation." We walked to the boxes sitting along the wall and opened the first one. Lana pulled several from the top and placed them in the scanner. Once they popped up on my computer, I forwarded them to her. "Stop by Taylor's desk. He saved the text messages. Send some of those along too."

Once I closed the lid, I turned, and Clement stared back at me. Without considering other options, I pulled the inventory binder out of my bag. I worked on the inventory for two hours, almost nearing the end. Lana reported the email to Tony is on its way. Then she sat in a chair facing my deck. "Bud told me about Clement's case. The missing ring sounds interesting. Have you found any other missing items?"

"No, I haven't. I'm almost at the end of the inventory list, and I've found nothing else missing. One picture shows a void between two items as if something were there, but I can't find it. Let me show you. You may see something I missed." I turned Lana's attention to my board. Then I pointed to the picture I referenced. "See this area. It appears large enough for an object to sit, but I have no record of it."

Lana studied the pictures for a minute, "I see what you mean. There was something in that place. Because nowhere else does he leave a void. His shelves were full of objects. Is that binder all of Clement's records? Could he have some older items that he failed to list in this inventory? Check through dad's old files."

Something stirred in my brain, but I couldn't pull it forward. "Thanks for the idea, Lana. Dad had old pictures at home from when Clement opened his shop too. I'll dig them out and compare them to what I see now. Perhaps something with jump out at me."

"Have you considered using the media to help find the ring? It might be a long shot because of the age, but it might be worth a try."

I nodded in agreement, "yes, I've considered it, but I wanted to complete the inventory list first. If I have multiple missing items, I'll include that one too."

My phone rang, so Lana hurried out the door. Mullins called for an update, but first, he asked about the tornado. I shared our experience with the fire and lightning victim. Then I moved into the situation with the receipts and text messages. "You mean these receipts might prove Margarite was part of a drug operation."

"We're not sure, but having coded receipts is strange. Has Margarite or Raul returned yet?"

"Neither one has shown at their house or work. It makes me wonder if they are dead too."

Our call lasted a little longer, but it yielded nothing of consequence. We're growing weary by the day. Something needs to pop in this case. We feel as if we're at a standstill. Some involved people are missing while others are dead. It makes investigating difficult if you can't ask questions to those that might help.

The afternoon settled, and Bud and I enjoyed grilling steaks for supper. We sat outside on the back porch and talked. We shared about our past, and we discussed our future. Bud clarified that our future is together.

Monday morning was hectic as my day started in the crime lab. The techs had already begun inspecting Jose's truck. Much to my surprise, they found a different fiber on the driver's seatbelt than what was in Tucker's vehicle. Also, a partial index fingerprint showed on the driver's door. I asked about drugs, and the answer was no. No drugs or drug residue was in the truck. With that, it disappointed me. Nevertheless, my thought process still considered drugs a possibility for the murders.

Since Mullins said yesterday, Raul and Maria are still missing. I want another crack at Rhett. Something connects this group of people, but what? Time for a bit of pushing and see what he tells me. I'll have a deputy pick him up, and I can ask my questions from our interrogation room,

I call for Tuttle and Taylor and ask them to meet in my office. Bud and Lana worked on the receipts in the corner. They asked for their four-year-old file from Louisiana in hopes of comparison.

The guys arrived minutes later. They acknowledged the other two but kept their attention on me. "Bring

Rhett in for additional questioning. I want to talk with him in the interrogation room. He knows more than he's offered so far, and now that his leg is healing, he should be able to answer questions without morphine."

"We'll pick him up and have him back here shortly. He shouldn't be able to put up a fuss since he can't walk without a cane." Tuttle said and chuckled as they left.

Maggie walked in right after the guys left, waving a piece of paper in the air. "Your lucky day, Sheriff." I cringed when she said it. How come I don't feel so lucky?

"Show me, Maggie." She handed the paper to me, and I grinned. "We have it in our hands, Maggie. Start the process today with the ads we prepared a few weeks ago. Thanks, Maggie."

Bud and Lana were watching our exchange. "What's so great, Sheriff?"

"We have the official document giving the Sheriff's Office authority to hire another deputy. We've been waiting on this for two years now. The county's population increases every year, but I worked with the same staff four years ago. It's about time. It would be nice to have a new hire within thirty days and trained in sixty. We would have extra staff for the holidays if I can make it happen."

"That's outstanding, Sheriff. Good luck with the search. Our Louisiana file is coming to our email soon. I think these receipts will match our file. If so, it might involve Margarite and Jose and a big drug dealer out of New Orleans. He runs dope using boats in the ocean. We hurt his stash when we busted a cargo ship, but we never got our hands on the dealer himself. His name is Pablo, with no last name. He never stays in one place longer than two days, and he travels across the southernmost parts of the country, and he has ties to Mexico."

"Wow, Lana. I didn't expect that. It would lend credence to the idea of drugs as the reason for murder. I'm waiting for the guys to bring Rhett in for questioning. He should be without his morphine pump now." I smile as I leave the office and head to the interview room, holding my folder. With Rhett sitting in the interrogation room alone, I peer through the two-way window at him. He seems a tad nervous already.

"Rhett. Thanks for waiting. I'll jump right in the questions. Are you familiar with a guy named Mateo Colon? He shot you. Look at this picture and tell me if you recognize him." I slid the photo across the table. Rhett leaned over and studied it while recognition spread across his face. I waited.

"I didn't know his name, but he was at the bar the night I got shot. His girlfriend waited at the bar for a drink right next to me. We started talking, and this guy didn't like it. I guess he took offense, so he shot me."

I nodded my head as he spoke. Then I started with my real reason for bringing him into the Sheriff's

Office. "Rhett, as I place photos on the table in front of you, let me know which people you recognize."

Every few seconds, I placed a photo on the table. Rhett takes his time at each one, but he ends knowing each one I laid out. Now, Rhett is friends with Raul, Maria, Jose, Margarite, Ava, and Angela. This makes for an exciting addition to my murder board. I pushed a little harder, and he admitted to being closer to Jose, Ava, and Angela. A friend introduced him to Ava and Angela. The friend's name is RT. That's all the information he has.

Rhett became flustered with my questions, so I stepped out of the room to give him time to calm. When I returned, I brought snacks. He gulped the water but broke small pieces off of the protein bar and chewed them slowly. While he continued working on his protein bar, I asked the name of his friend again, RT. He swears he doesn't know it and becomes hostile by yelling obscenities. Then Taylor enters the room without knocking. He never says a word, just stands by the door with his arms folded. Rhett quietens.

"One last question, Rhett, then Taylor will drive you home. Where are Raul Diaz and Maria Jorge staying? They could be in grave danger if they're not located."

He looked at me with wild eyes, "Why would I tell you if I knew? Are you grilling them too? Better yet, what do they have to do with anything?"

"Their friends, Jose and Margarite, are dead. Someone shot them in the head and tossed them into the lake. That's why we want to find them."

The information shocked him. He had no words. Once he collected himself, "I'm not sure where Raul and Maria are, Sheriff. I haven't spoken to them for weeks. Raul has family in Louisiana. Can I go now?" My head spun when he mentioned Louisiana. Are they hiding in Louisiana?

Rhett stood and limped to the door while Taylor held it open for him. Taylor drove him home, and once he was in his car alone, he called. "Sheriff, do you think Maria and Raul are in Louisiana? That might be the connection to this whole mess."

"My thoughts too. Bud and Lana are on a conference call with Tony on the receipts. When they're free, I'm sharing our conversation with Rhett. Come back to the office when you can."

While I waited for Bud and Lana to end their call, I pondered the Louisiana connection. Raul has family there, Bud and Lana worked a drug case there, now we have coded receipts in Raul's apartment. Did Raul and Maria involve Margarite and Jose in the drug business? If so, who shot Margarite and Jose, and why? Why are Raul and Maria on the run?

This case has too many unknowns. We should have solved this thing by now. Instead, we still have nothing with Raul and Maria on the run, four murders, and no ID on the cap-wearing guy. I glance at my notes. Circled in the upper right-hand corner of a page is a reminder.

I grabbed my desk phone and dialed the lab. Harold answered, and I explained what I needed. "I have the prints right here, Sheriff. This morning, I confirmed the partial from Jose's truck, and the part from the shell casing is a match. Unfortunately, the fingerprint isn't in AFIS. The print owner has never been in the service or arrested. However, the good news is when you capture them, I can match it to the truck and the casing."

Once I lay the phone in its cradle, my head falls back on my chair. I reviewed what I know now. Once I find the fingerprint owner, I can prove they shot McAlister and drove Jose's truck. So, I can place them at two crimes, but it doesn't help Tucker and Mary Lou's murder.

Lana walks into the office, holding two cups of coffee. "I hope one of those is mine," I said with a grin. "I could use it. This case gets stranger by the minute."

"What happened with Rhett's interview? Did he give you some information you can use?"

"Yes, he did. It will interest you and Bud, too. Where is Bud? I'd like to share it with you both. We might have another aspect of this case to work."

Bud strolls in holding two cups of coffee, and both ladies laugh. "Lana beat me to it, huh?" He chuckles, knowing I'll drink both cups. "Let's hear your updates."

Over the next few minutes, I shared details of Rhett's interview. The duo asked questions when they needed clarification, and they listened when they didn't. Toward the end of the conversation, Bud knew I was holding back. "What else did you discover, Sheriff? You haven't told us all of it."

Chapter 13

My eyes turn up, and I grin, playing it up for them. "The biggest piece of information is Raul Diaz has family in Louisiana. Rhett seemed to think Raul and Maria fled to his family. Now, share with me about your discussion with Tony."

"The coded receipts are the same as the ones we found in Louisiana. If Raul has family in Louisiana, and the receipts match, I say Raul is running drugs for a family member. With a last name like Diaz, there will be too many to check without a semblance of a location. Can we find Angela Diaz and question her? She is Raul's sister, right?"

As I turned a few pages in my book, I sipped my coffee. It was hot, just the way I like it. "Here it is. Angela Diaz is JoJo's girlfriend and Raul's sister. Here's her number too. Let me try to reach her and see if she will come to the office for a chat."

One button after another, I dialed her number. In an unbelievable turn, Angela answered the phone. Based on recent events, I figured she would ignore my call. The explanation I provided for our meeting spurred activity. She stated she would be at the office in thirty minutes.

While we waited, we devised a plan. We needed Angela to talk about her brother. She sounded scared when I mentioned Raul's name. Almost as if he kept her in the dark about his plans. We'll ask her about his plans and get her reaction. Lana is good with reading people, and she can tell if Angela is lying. I can't arrest Angela for lying, but I can make it difficult while she's in custody.

Angela arrived on time. Her face showed signs of anguish, with black circles under her eyes. Since I don't know Angela, I'm unsure if that is a typical look for her or if she's gone without sleep. We sit across from each other, and I start the interview. Bud and Lana are on the other side of the wall, watching me through a two-way window.

The interview started with me offering her food or drink. She declined, so I pressed forward. Several times and in a different context, I asked about Raul. Angela never faltered as her answer was always the same. She has no clue where her brother is or who he is with. She assumes Maria is with him, but she has no way to confirm it. Neither of them answers their cell phones. She's at a loss.

When I asked about the coded receipts found in Raul's house, she repeated she didn't know about those. If she's familiar with them, I don't have a way to prove it.

Then I asked about the Louisiana relations. She didn't hold back and said they have cousins in Eden Isle, but she doesn't think Raul would go back there since one of our cousins tried to sweet talk Maria into dating him instead of Raul. Raul got mad, and he hadn't seen their cousins in a few years.

"Is there anywhere between Georgia and Louisiana that he might visit? Sheriff Mullins has their house and their workplaces under surveillance. Neither one has shown their faces at either place." I leaned back in my chair and gave her time to think. When she didn't offer an idea, I pushed again on the receipts. Nothing came of that question, either.

As I walked her out the door, I said, "by the way, do you have a contact number for your cousin? I'd like to check with him and make sure Raul is not there."

Angela stopped and stared at me, relenting by texting me a contact card. She acted like she wanted to escape the confines of the interview room, and the quickest way to do that was to provide me a contact number.

After she left, I met Lana and Bud in my office. "Angela provided little information, but she sent me her cousin's contact card. Now, let me see if he answers the phone."

Within seconds I dialed the number for Tito Jersey, or TJ, as they call him. Someone answers with 'yes' for a greeting. I tell him my name, and he pauses, not sure how to respond. Since I hear nothing, I ask about Raul and say I want to keep Raul safe. To do that, I need his location. Silence lingers, but there is movement. It might be TJ shifting in his seat, or he may communicate with someone else.

"Uh, Sheriff. I'm not sure where Raul is right now. I'll check around and call you back."

Then a dial tone blared in my ear. And that made me mad.

"I need someone to ping this cell phone number. Taylor is in the field. Bud, can you do that?" I pleaded because I wanted to know if this guy was sitting in Eden Isle, Louisiana.

"Give me the number. I'll be back in a second." Bud trots out the office door on a mission.

Lana looks at me, "Eden Isle sits on the water's edge. It would be a simple spot to move drugs by boat along the southern seaboard."

"Let's see what Bud finds out before you pack your bags. That's a long way to travel if it's not needed." I stated more for myself than hers. More time away from each other doesn't sound appealing.

Bud appeared in the doorway with a grin. "Eden Isle it is. The only cell tower around Eden Isle pinged. I've placed a call into the Louisiana FBI office. We're on standby for a trip, depending on what they can pull together for us."

My head bobs as an acknowledgment while I study the notes on my desk. The case has so many loopholes. I wanted to make sure we closed them all. If Margarite and Jose are dead because of the drug business with Raul, who killed Tucker and Mary Lou? That still bothers me. I find no reason for Tucker or Mary Lou's death. Were they in the wrong place at the wrong time?

The time of day prevented me from thinking about this case. My brain is too tired to concentrate. "I'm hungry. Are you ready to eat? Let's call Taylor and see if he can break for food. Nothing has come over the radios in a while."

Thirty minutes later, we sat two by two in a booth in my favorite diner. A thick juicy hamburger is just what I needed. The food in this place always makes me feel better. While we chewed, Taylor explained he thought he was close to finding something on Margarite and Jose's text messages. He should finish the report tonight.

Taylor gave me hope something else would pop overnight. I remembered Mullins didn't call me today for an update, and I wasn't proactive in calling him either. I'll make that happen first thing in the morning. My plans for the day changed when we interviewed Angela. I hadn't expected that interview, but I'm glad we did it. Now, we have Raul's location. One step closer to finding out the truth.

Tuesday rolled around with pleasant weather as Bud and Lana left for Louisiana. I wanted to tag along but knew I couldn't, so my mood dampened as I waved at them. Taylor stood beside me, which made their leaving bearable. As soon as they turned out of the parking lot, Taylor leaned into my ear, "I have a present for you. Come on."

I turned to answer, but he was halfway to the door. "A present? That sounds ominous coming from you." Then, when he glanced over his shoulder, he grinned.

We entered my office, and his computer sat on the plastic table. He lifted the lid to reveal a page with squiggly lines. "That's my present. Taylor, what on earth is that?" I pointed to his laptop and squished my nose.

"This is proof Margarite and Jose sold drugs. One of their text messages from their cellphones had a hyperlink embedded in it. I clicked it, and it directed me to a chatroom. This chatroom has multiple users, and it has been active for years. Luckily for us, I located Margarite and Jose's screen names from their phones. Otherwise, I'm not sure we would have found them."

"So, what did you find in this chatroom?" My pulse quickened when I realized where the information could lead.

"The chatroom gave us the proof we need for the drug sales, and I found the IP address for Margarite and Jose. It led me to their front door. If Bud and Lana can find Raul and Maria, I would have proved it involves them too." Taylor leaned back in the chair, locked his fingers, and placed his hands behind his head with a smug look on his face.

"That's great work, Taylor. But what about tying Tucker and Mary Lou to this drug mess?" I lifted an eyebrow as I sat back. Taylor shifted in his chair, looked at the laptop, then back up at me.

"I can't do that, Sheriff. There's no record of Tucker or Mary Lou anywhere. It doesn't mention them in the chatroom or the texts. But there are many texts from an individual with the initials RT and another from CU. I don't know anyone with those initials," His eyebrows bunched. He runs his hands through

142

his hair and lets out a sigh. "I didn't do as well as I thought."

"You did good, Taylor, but the case isn't over yet because we must find CU and RT now. I can't let Tucker and Mary Lou's murder go unpunished, that's all. We must keep plugging because I'm just not sure the murders are all about the drugs. It doesn't sit well with me."

Taylor provided new information on the case. This information will give the district attorney a solid case for the county. The chatroom documents, along with the IP address proof, are indisputable evidence. So what makes little sense are Tucker and Mary Lou's deaths? Why? Why would someone kill them?

Once I updated my notes, I called Mullins. I'm not sure how much help he has been on the case, but I'm obligated to call. Mullins answers on the first ring, which I found odd. We talked for thirty minutes as I shared our updates. He seemed fine until I mentioned the guys with the initials RT and CU. Then, Mullins turned silent. After a ten-second delay, I asked if he was still on the line. He answered by saying he'd call me back.

The call ended so quickly that it bewildered me. Why would he hang up so fast after I brought up RT and CU? Does he know guys with those initials? If so, who are they?

"Taylor, can you come to my office and bring your laptop?" I had an idea.

He entered within seconds. "What's up, Sheriff?"

"I updated Mullins on our findings, and when I mentioned the guys with the initials CU and RT, he grew silent. Is there a way to determine if RT or CU is in the chatroom or just in the text messages? If we can find the chatroom correspondence, it might lead to a friend or someone with knowledge of their names."

"After we spoke, I went back to the text messages from RT and CU. Neither one has a contact card on either Jose's or Margarite's cell phones. The number used to text is a prepaid burner phone. They used the phone for a while, then tossed it." Taylor's fingers flew across his keypad. It astonished me because I did not know he could type that fast.

Maggie walked into my office, carrying a folder of papers. She grinned as she placed them in the center of my desk. "What is this, Maggie?" I asked, trying to contain my annoyance at the interruption.

"This is your applications for the open position at the Sheriff's Office. There are thirty-one so far. As they come in, I'll place them in the folder on top. Happy hunting, Sheriff."

"Thirty-one people want to be a deputy in this county. I've never dreamed that many would apply." I flipped through the applicants as I considered the process. The more I thought about it, the more it seemed a rather daunting project.

"Sheriff, let me do some digging on the chatroom information for you. You have fun with the applicants." Taylor grabbed his laptop and bolted for the door. He wanted nothing to do with this.

A few of the applicants looked promising, and for that, I was grateful. I write a note to work through these this week and prepare for interviews the following week. I marked several to review, and I shoved the folder to the side. When I glanced up, I looked at Clement's photo, still taped to the middle of the murder board.

Since I had a break on the murders, I pulled the inventory log binder out of my desk. I thumbed the remaining pages, telling myself I still had several hours of inventory to weed through. I took it upon myself to work on it for one hour. Then I would meet with Taylor on his findings. However, time flew, and when my eyes needed a break, it was two hours later. Just as I was picking up the phone for Taylor, a dispatcher sent him to an auto accident.

I walked to the coffee bar and helped myself to a large cup of the hottest coffee in the county. As I added creamer to my coffee, Bud called my cell phone. He explains their plans for tonight. The FBI has a location in Eden Isle under surveillance, and they'll execute a warrant tonight. I told him to be safe and to call when it was over.

Now, the wait is on again. I'm waiting for Taylor to end his accident investigation and Bud's search warrant to end. While waiting, I call McAlister and check in on his recovery. All seems well there, except it will take a long road for him to return to the DNR. He'll endure many months of physical therapy, but he's a healthy guy, so the PT shouldn't bother him too much.

My desk phone rang as I ended the call with McAlister. I listened to Mullins as he apologized for the earlier call. Investigator Davis came into his office with an urgent issue. More chatter is on the streets about a hit, and there's still no target mentioned, just the threat. Some of Rafael's guys were at the bar at the county line, mouthing off about police meddling in their affairs.

I leaned back in my chair, considering our options for the threat. "Do you see any of those guys shooting one of our deputies? If so, I'm pulling mine from the street. They can work from the office and answer calls in pairs." My shoulders and neck hurt. A knot formed on the top of my shoulder, and I rubbed it with all my might, trying to ease the tension.

Mullins hemmed and hawed about the chatter. Finally, he confirmed the chatter mentions no one by name. After my comments, he considers doing the same with his deputies. As our call ended, Mullins received a call from dispatch stating he had an auto accident involving a deputy. I listened to the message as he ended our call.

An auto accident involving a deputy. Could that result from Rafael's chatter? I picked up the radio and asked all deputies to report to the office. I couldn't take the chance of losing one of mine. Two deputies were in the bullpen filling out reports, and they stuck their heads in my office. I filled them on the situation, and they agreed to pair. They are to remain in pairs until I tell them otherwise.

The same conversation took place a few more times before all the deputies had a partner and knew the drill. Taylor and Tuttle are paired, and they are my partners. I asked Taylor not to mention anything to Lana. Bud and Lana would find out when they returned home. "Are you sure, Sheriff? If things go south, that will be a hard explanation."

"Blame it on me, Taylor. They have enough problems with the search warrant tonight."

"What search warrant?" Taylor looked at me with creases on his forehead.

"They are executing a search warrant in Eden Isle tonight looking for Raul and Maria. Bud said he would call afterward." Deep down, I prayed for their safety. I've seen bad things happen during search warrants.

At home, I walked the floor because Bud and Lana were part of the team executing the search warrant. Bud didn't tell me what time, so I paced. For some reason, I couldn't contain my nerves. Taylor called twice, already asking if I had any news, which didn't ease my concern. The last time I looked at the clock, it was approaching two in the morning.

The phone call came at 4:05 AM. Bud described the chaos that ensued once they pounded on the door. Bullets flew at breakneck speed from both sides of the door. Someone struck Raul in the lower abdomen. Maria remained unscathed, just scared and worried about Raul. With Raul in surgery, Bud and Lana sat with Maria in the surgery waiting room. Once Raul was out of surgery and in recovery, we transported Maria to a warehouse the FBI discovered.

Bud continued with his story because I had no questions. He informed me the FBI found an address in Raul's possession. When they checked it, it was an abandoned warehouse on the outskirts of Eden Isle. They placed Tito Jersey under arrest for drug possession and distribution. This is the same group he and Lana looked for over four years ago. The crime lab is dusting for prints. If Raul's and Maria's fingerprints are in the warehouse, we have plenty of evidence against them to send to jail.

When Bud took a break from speaking, all I asked was, "when are you coming home?"

Bud chuckled, "as soon as we can. We'd like to bring Raul and Maria back to Georgia with us. But we'll see how things play out today. We're unsure if Raul's health would prevent him from traveling. One other thing, Lana spoke with Maria, and Maria denied the drugs. When Lana asked why they left, Maria told her they thought someone would kill them too. Jose and Margarite were their friends. She couldn't explain their murder, but Lana thinks Maria is holding back."

Once our call ended, I couldn't sleep because my mind raced in a thousand directions. If Maria thought someone would target them for murder, she suspects something. They are part of a bigger group, and we just haven't found it yet.

Chapter 14

In the office, Taylor stuck his head through the doorway, "Any other updates besides the 4:00 AM call?"

I glanced up at him, "Nope. Nothing. It's early out there. They'll call in an hour. Their night was longer than ours." My cell phone rang while Taylor was present. I waved him in when I recognized the caller.

"Good Morning, Sheriff Mullins. How's your deputy?" I asked because I wouldn't want to be in his shoes.

Mullins shared the news the deputy remains in the hospital but should recover. The deputy chased Mateo Colon, and they both crashed into the woods. The hospital released Mateo into their custody late last night. He admitted to shooting Rhett because Rhett talked to his girlfriend at our famous bar.

"You have Mateo in custody. That's splendid news, Sheriff. What charges are you pursuing if you don't mind my asking?" I winked at Taylor, waiting for an answer.

"We have him on aggravated assault and a parole violation. He's going back to jail." Mullins stated, then he asked about Bud and Lana. I filled him in on the warrant from last night. He agrees Maria is holding onto more information than she's sharing.

"Sheriff, have we compared Maria and Raul's prints to the prints from the truck and the shell casing? It would help rule them out as suspects in the murders."

"No, we haven't. Bud said the FBI printed Raul and Maria, and they'll compare their prints to the ones found in the warehouse. That information will be forthcoming today."

A little before lunch, Bud calls, and we exchange small talk. He's trying to ease the distance, but I want to solve the case. So, I push forward on the prints since he has the answers I need. "Raul and Maria were in the warehouse. We found their prints in the area holding the drugs, and someone wrote their names on a pad of paper in an office area. But we're unsure what the list of the name represents. The FBI team seems to think the names on the list are their runners. Now, to find the people on the list."

"Can you forward Raul and Maria's fingerprints to me? Taylor and I want to compare them to the partial prints from the truck and the shell casing. If nothing else, to rule them out as the murderers."

"Coming to you now. We're on our way to the hospital to see Raul. He's awake. I'll call later and let you know how that goes." Bud made a kissing sound into the phone. I chuckled as my email tone sounded. Since Harold is waiting for the email, I forwarded the prints directly to him for comparison.

With Taylor hanging on every word, I share my conversation with Bud. Then I tell Taylor I'm interviewing candidates this afternoon and stay close to the office if he can. I'll let him speak with the candidate if they pass my interview. Taylor walks back to the bullpen and dives into the chatroom again.

The afternoon was a blur with the interviews. One candidate was promising, and since he knows the area, that's a significant plus. The other three were not what I was looking for in a deputy. I want this one to fit in with the group. A Sheriff's Office is no place for drama. Everyone must get along with the others. It's not expected everyone agrees on everything, but they have to support it.

Taylor met with the potential candidate. They spent more than an hour together, so I knew he passed Taylor's test. I waited in the office until Taylor wrapped up his interview. As the door opened, I stood, and both men were comfortable with each other. That told me a lot. I shook the guy's hand and told him we would be in touch.

After the guy left, we met in my office and discussed his interviews. Both of us agreed. Braxton Long was the top on our list. But we spoke with more applicants, just to be sure. "I was hoping for more diversity in my next hire. We've never hired a female deputy since I came on board. Why is that Taylor?"

"I can't answer for you, Sheriff. With his ethnicity being African American, Braxton is your diversity hire, even though we have other ethnicities working here too. He's a big guy too. We could use the help in warrants and such. Braxton played college ball intending to play for the NFL, but when his dad died unexpectedly from a heart attack, he came home to take care of his mother and younger sister."

"He sounds like a good hire. Braxton has a servant's heart, and that's what we need around here. I get the diversity hire, but I was thinking another female around here would be nice." I grinned, but I meant what I said. A woman would join this department sometime during my tenure.

Taylor chuckles as he turns toward the door, "I'm heading home for a few hours of rest since I'm working the night shift."

"Thanks, Taylor. I appreciate your help." I say to his back as my desk phone rings.

Harold explains he compared Maria and Raul's prints to the shell casing and the truck, and they are not a match. Of course, I wasn't expecting them to match, but it's nice to have it confirmed. So, whose prints are those?

As I glance at the clock, my stomach rumbles. I realize I haven't eaten or left the building today. It's time for food. But before I leave, I called Rhett and gave him the news his shooter sat in jail. When he answered, the background noise was so loud, I had a hard time hearing him. I yelled into the phone about Mateo, saying he didn't know anyone by that name. In between our responses, I heard someone shout RT. I asked Rhett about knowing someone that uses the initials RT or CU. He denied it, then I asked about someone there saying RT, and he corrected me. Rhett says there is a guy named Artie that works here.

When Rhett said he was working, I asked him where. He talked around me as if he didn't want to say. As I pushed harder, he said he was working for a friend. Then Rhett spoke to someone and said he had to end the call.

Now, my interest piques. Where is Rhett, and what is he doing? Did that person say RT or Artie, as Rhett said? Is Rhett covering for someone? Time to put a surveillance unit on Rhett. I want to know everything about this guy.

Since Taylor is working the night shift, I'll ask him to investigate Rhett. I want it all, from work to girlfriends to his checking account balance. He's up to something, and I bet he knows Mateo. For some reason, he acted as if he overlooked the shooter's name. Tomorrow, we can begin Rhett's surveillance.

My thoughts turned to Clement and Lana's suggestion. Once I finish the inventory, I'll ask the media for help in locating the ring. If I'm lucky, someone in the county wears this ring, and I'm hopeful they'll come forward. The ring's owner will give me a lead into how they came to own it. Now, to get home and search dad's photos of Clement's store.

Photos from dad's stash covered my bed. While I searched for the store photos, I took a trip down memory lane. Birthday parties, fishing trips to school basketball games, Dad was always there, cheering me on no matter the circumstance. Then my mind gravitated to Lana, and I wondered how her childhood was with just a mom. I would have liked to have met our mom. It's strange how she died not too long after dad. Cancer won the war with her.

My cellphone rang, and I had to dig it out of my pants pocket. Bud told me about their win and how Raul and Maria are returning to Georgia with them. In two days, he would be home. We would house Raul in our jail until charges were official. Then, when we convict him, we'll transfer him to federal lockup. Charges are pending for Maria. Our call ended with idle chitchat about nothing, but it felt good.

As I laid the phone on my nightstand, my eyes discovered a photo that had slipped off the bed. This is the one I was searching for all this time. Dad and Clement stood in front of Clement's counter while the newspaper photographer takes a photo. Clement supported dad in his run for Sheriff, and this was the article. Unfortunately, the paper turned a dingy shade of yellow over the years. I set it off to the side, wondering if Harold had any magic for yellow newsprint.

With the night shift starting soon, I called Taylor. He was already at the office, set to finish the chatroom conversations. "Taylor, I have something new to occupy your time tonight. I want a full workup on Rhett. Get whatever you can find from the office tonight. Tomorrow we'll begin surveillance on him. I want to know where he's working and for whom."

A tinge of excitement sounded in Taylor's voice. "Thanks, Sheriff. I'll get started right away. I'll stay around in the morning until you come in so we can discuss my findings."

Deputy Damon Taylor and Deputy Brock Tuttle are two of the best people in the world. They have my back no matter what. I hope our next hire is the same. I laid back on my pillows, rehashing my conversation with Braxton, and nothing jumped at me. So why am I stalling? Is it because I'm scared to change the dynamic at the office?

The stars twinkled in the night sky when I awoke from a deep sleep. I didn't wake up all night because I was so tired. But I'm eager for Taylor's results from the Rhett investigation. My bones tell me Rhett is mixed up in this mess somehow.

When I arrived at the office, Taylor was out answering an alarm call at a local business. I radioed him and advised my status. He responded by stating someone broke a window at the cellphone store, but they took nothing he could see. The manager is on his way in to confirm.

It was quiet in the office at this time of day. This might be my new favorite time to be in the office. Clement's inventory list remained open on my desk. I placed the two newspaper pictures inside the binder for safekeeping. While Taylor was away, I plugged along on the inventory, turning to the last page in the inventory list. The first item on the page was missing from the photos. So much for luck. Now, a gold statue with ruby eyes is missing.

Considering the uniqueness of each piece, could they be with the same family? What are the odds someone stole a diamond ring and a statue with ruby eyes? As I reached for the phone to call Harold, Taylor entered. "Are you ready for me, Sheriff? I've got good stuff."

With those comments, I replaced the receiver on the cradle and grabbed a notepad. "Let's hear what you found out on Rhett."

Taylor pulls his notes out of a folder and separates them into piles. "We'll start with banking. Rhett has $24,010.88 in his checking account, with another $77 342.00 in savings." My mouth dropped open, but I didn't stop Taylor from questioning it.

"During some months, Rhett makes large deposits, but nothing larger than $6,000 at a time. My guess is to avoid the feds. The money is cash, never checks. He has lived alone since his last girlfriend moved out on him about three months ago. They had a joint account, but it has since been closed." Taylor paused while he shifted his notes.

"All of his bills are current, not that he has many. He pays his bills through the bank's online bill pay service, and he makes some deposits with a teller, while others through the ATM. We have no way to find out where he gets his money unless he fesses up, or we follow him."

"We need to find out how a guy like Rhett has that much money. It's illegal. I just don't know where he gets it from yet. The only cash businesses I'm aware of are selling drugs and gambling. So, to find out, surveillance starts tonight. I'll take the first shift." I glanced at the notes again. This confirms my feelings. Rhett is up to no good.

I left the office in search of downtime before Rhett's surveillance begins tonight. Rhett lives in a familiar area, but I want a quick look around before night falls. Twenty minutes later, I pass his apartment. He lives in a well-worn apartment complex on the south side of town. Boards cover some of the windows, while others have hanging flower baskets on their porches. Rhett pulled his blinds, so I can't tell if he's inside.

With the lingering thought of Rhett being at home, I drive to the rear of the complex. The back looks eerily similar to the front side but with more people. There is a group of people sitting in a circle in the common area. One points the finger at me and waves. I casually nod while my insides quiver. Do they know why I'm riding around their lot? I continue around the lot, returning to the front of the complex. I note no changes at Rhett's apartment, so I leave the lot and head for home.

Once I reach home, I draw out the parking lot and Rhett's apartment location on a napkin which is the first piece of paper I find. Then I decided on two areas that would provide adequate coverage for surveillance. In preparation, I change into all black pants, a shirt, and a jacket. On the way out the door, I grab my black cap.

Taylor is the only person who knows I plan on watching Rhett tonight. He'll be ready if I need help. I parked my vehicle in the parking lot behind Rhett's apartment complex. This gives me visual access from my car, and I can watch from behind a rock wall if I need to move around.

A light burns in the apartment right inside the front door. Now, I wish I had the layout of the apartment. It looks like the front door leads to the family room, then the kitchen to the right side. Every so often, a shadow passes in front of the front door. With someone in the apartment, it's time to get comfortable. I have to talk myself into being patient. Patience is a constant battle for me.

Since I turned my volume down on my phone, I peek at it inside my bag for fear of the light shining through the woods. Two hours into the surveillance, Rhett steps outside his door, turns around and closes the door, making sure he locked it. He glances back and forth across the lot as he walks to his truck. Does he suspect someone is watching him?

Rhett wears nice clothes. But when Mateo shot him, he wore old jeans and an older T-shirt. This is a change. Wonder why? Rhett slides into the front seat and checks himself in the mirror. Then, he backs out of his space and drives out of the lot in the opposite direction.

Once I start my car, I have to hurry to catch up with Rhett. He crosses the county line into Mullins county. Then I chastised myself because I didn't consider this turn of events. I pressed Mullins's speed dial and waited. He answered after several rings.

"Sheriff, this is Sheriff Steele. I'm tailing Rhett Welsh in your county. He's driving a late model Toyota truck, navy. I wanted you to be aware."

"Thanks, Sheriff, for the update. Do you require help? I can help or send a deputy."

"No help needed. I'm trying to figure out what this guy does for a living. He has more money in his bank account than I do, and he makes large cash deposits. So we thought surveillance would help explain our questions."

"Okay, Sheriff. Be safe out there and call if you need anything." Sheriff Mullins ended the call.

As soon as our call ended, I watched Rhett answer his cell phone, and I had a strange sensation pass through my mind. My next call was to Taylor. "Taylor, it's me. Can you pull phone records for Rhett's cell phone? I just witnessed a coincidence, and I don't believe in those." I continued behind Rhett as he cruised around both counties. He stopped for food but nothing else.

"Sure, I can. I'll pull them first thing in the morning before I go on patrol. Are you going to share what you witnessed?" Curious about her request, Taylor asked because they don't have a warrant for Rhett's phone records.

"Not yet. I don't want to incriminate anyone until I have proof. Let me know when you get it. Thanks, Taylor." When our call ends, I place my cell in the console as we drive circles around two counties. This is awkward. How come I feel like Rhett knows I'm following him? That's why he isn't stopping anywhere meaningful.

Chapter 15

As Rhett turns right into his apartment complex, I continue straight. I turned my headlights off as I turned into the parking lot next to his complex. When I reached my hideout, I exited the car. We've driven around for hours, and I needed to stretch. Before I made it to my hideout, Rhett entered his apartment. Or at least I can say the light is on the inside. Now, I wonder if he gave me the slip.

A minute later, my phone vibrates in my pocket. Mullins wants my location. I paused before I texted back, "on my way home." Then I questioned my intent as I climbed into my car and settled in for a little longer. Most of the time, my gut is right, and right now, my intuition is telling me something will happen in this parking lot within thirty minutes.

Well, I can read Mullins like a book. Twenty-eight minutes after the text, an older model SUV pulls to the curb at Rhett's apartment. The driver faced the apartment, leaving me no view. Rhett waited for them by the door because the driver never stepped foot out of the vehicle. Instead, Rhett approached the car, holding nothing I could see from my vantage point. They spoke briefly, then Rhett walked back inside with nothing visible in his hands.

Who's driving the SUV? Is it Mullins or one of his flunkies? I couldn't read the license plate or see the driver, but they knew that. They planned for it to happen just like that, which makes me mad.

Once I realized my night was over, I drove home with a million things coursing through my mind, like Sheriff Mullins' involvement with Rhett, and if so, how? Thinking back on my conversation with Mullins, I remembered he grew quiet when asked about CU and RT. Are they a part of his gang?

Tomorrow is just a few short hours away. Sleep took over before I knew it. Then the dreams came one after another. Dad showed in a few, then Lana lying in a hospital bed, Bud smiling. I sunk a little deeper into my bed until my sheriff's office radio toned four beeps. In this county, that's serious.

I ran to the radio and grab the mic and yelled for dispatch. The response scared me to death. "Repeat that, dispatch."

"Sheriff, someone torched the side yard of the office. It's burning close to the building. So we're moving the prisoners to other cells until the fire department arrives."

"I'm on my way." As I ran into my room, I dressed in my clothes from last night since they lay on the floor by the bed. It took too much energy to toss them in the hamper. My hair was still somewhat in a ponytail, even if it was a little crooked. I grabbed my cell phone with my finger poised over Taylor's number.

"Taylor, we have an incident at the office. What's your status?"

I waited as I listened to loud noises. "I'm at the office, Sheriff. It's bad. But the fire department arrived within minutes of the call. From where I stand, they saved the building, but not the yard."

"I'll be there in ten minutes." With the car pointed to the Sheriff's office, I pressed the gas pedal to the floor. My sirens blared, and I swerved in and out of traffic. I could see the smoke for miles before I took the last turn into the lot. How could someone do this so close to downtown? Wouldn't someone have seen them do it?

Taylor joins me on the sidewalk as we gawk at the damage. The fire department did a fantastic job saving the building and the people inside. That was my biggest concern. Now, I pulled Taylor off to the side and shared my concerns.

By the time I finished with Taylor, his mouth hung open in disbelief. "Sheriff, I can't believe it, but it shouldn't surprise me. Sheriff Mullins has been all in our investigation. His goal was to find out what we had on his crew. My next task is the phone records. However, if he's halfway intelligent, he'll use a burner phone. If he does, our workload just became harder."

Lieutenant Carlson of the fire department strolls our way. "Sheriff, we extinguished the fire, but we have to clean up the mess. As soon as I find the origin, I'll let you know. Also, you might get a look at the instigator from the camera on the corner."

"Thanks, Lieutenant. I'll be waiting for your findings." I answered quickly so I could answer my ringing phone.

"Sheriff Steele." When I hear the caller, I pause and take in the sound of his voice. "Hey, Bud. You're missing all the action. Someone torched the common area at the office. There were no injuries, but the yard sustained heavy damage."

Taylor watched and listened as I spoke with Bud. His face had the look of a hopeful schoolboy waiting on his date, then several minutes into the call, Taylor's cellphone rang, and he stepped away to answer. He spoke in whispered tones to his caller, who I assumed was Lana.

Once we finished our calls, we entered the office together. We split at the door. I strolled to the coffee bar while Taylor walked to the bullpen. Taylor enjoyed the computer side of investigations, which I was glad. I knew what I needed, just not sure how to get the results.

While Taylor poured over Sheriff Mullins' cell phone calls, I worked on Clement's case again. The end was so close I could see it. With only a few lines remaining in the inventory, I could knock it out in no time, and that's what I did. When I put a red check mark beside the last entry, I wanted to jump and down. Now, I discovered two missing items. It's the diamond ring and the gold statue with ruby eyes. With Bud and Lana coming home in the morning, I'll discuss my next steps with Lana before moving forward. I liked her idea of using the media.

Since the inventory was complete, I felt a sense of relief because I had direction on Clement's case, hoping someone would recognize the items. If someone comes forward, I'll have a new avenue to investigate and possibly find a murderer.

Another trip to the coffee bar, and Sheriff Mullins walked into my office. When I saw his face, he stopped by to garner any news from last night. I was ready for him. He acknowledged me by my title, and I did the same. Then he bombarded me with questions. What happened last night? Did you find out anything important? Where did Rhett stop?

Lifting my hand to slow him down, I said, "Sheriff. I learned nothing last night. It was a complete waste of time. We drove around two counties for hours with no stops. It's like he knew I was tailing him. Last night was strange. Have you found out anything new?"

"Nope. Nothing. My deputy is home now, recovering from the car crash. Oh, well. I thought I would stop in and see how your night transpired. Do you want me to handle the surveillance tonight?" He lowered his eyes to his hands as he asked the question.

"No, I don't think that will be necessary, Sherriff. I haven't decided if I'll continue watching Rhett. I'm meeting with my guys today. If I change my mind, I'll call."

Mullins turns and walks out the door, but not before stopping and looking at me over his shoulder. He's trying to decide if I'm speaking the truth about Rhett. I gave him no sign not to believe me, but some people just have that intuition. I let him leave, then I called for Taylor.

"What's he doing here?" Taylor asks, nodding his head toward Mullins with a scowl on his face.

"He stopped in to see if I learned anything new last night. This mess involves Mullins. I just have to prove it. There was no other reason for him to be in this county today."

Taylor nods in agreement, then explains his findings. "I've had no luck on the cellphone records. If Mullins made a call to Rhett, it's from a burner phone, and it's possible both used a burner phone last night." He fingers a few pieces of paper. "Rhett didn't make a deposit last night as he has on the same night for months. You made him change his routine."

I rubbed my temples on both sides of my head. "I need a car, an unknown car. Surveillance won't work in my car again. He would notice that one again. I'm going back tonight." Taylor is staring at me. "What's wrong?"

"Number one, you're not going alone, especially since we suspect Sheriff Mullins. Number two, I got a car we can use. My tow truck driver CI has a sweet ride at the impound yard. I'll call him, and we can go pick it up before he leaves for the night." Taylor grins because he feels like he solved the world's problems. He didn't solve the world's problems, but he solved mine.

The rest of the day was rapid-fire. I handled citizen complaints of a trashy house, car racing, and a barking dog. Complaints always come in threes. Once those were off my desk, I moved to Braxton. I reviewed his file once more and still liked what I saw. With two more candidates coming in today for interviews, I should have my answer by tonight.

I glanced at the clock and noticed I barely had time for a quick sandwich before my first interview today. I nodded at Clement's picture as I left the office like he knew I was close to solving his murder.

The first interview was a colossal waste of time. This guy's head was so big it barely fit through the door. He kept repeating how good he was at everything. I didn't have time to ask many questions because he never stopped talking. When our time ended, I escorted him out of the office as fast as I could. The second interview turned out well. If I hadn't set my heart on Braxton, I would have chosen this one. After the interviews were complete, I dialed Braxton and offered him a Sheriff's Deputy position. He accepted the position and agreed to start on Monday.

Another load lifted from my shoulders, and I liked the feeling. Now to finish this investigation, as Dante's warning still resonates in my brain. My two weeks are almost over, and I wonder what his warning meant. What does he plan to do if we don't solve the murders in two weeks?

On my way out of the office, I updated Taylor and Tuttle on the new hire. They were happy to hear relief was on the way. Both guys will stop in the office tomorrow when Braxton comes by to fill out paperwork. Then I mentioned to Taylor I would be at home without giving their plans away to Tuttle. The less that knew they were watching Rhett, the better.

Taylor picked me up from my house, and we headed to Rhett's. This car is a gray four-door sedan. The car windows hold no tint, which makes a stakeout difficult. Anyone that looks inside the car can see us and, in an instant, figure out what we are doing.

On our arrival, Rhett's vehicle remained in the same spot as last night. The apartment light continues to burn. We slumped in the car seats and placed the binoculars level with the dash, hoping it would obscure our look. At midnight, we discuss options. Rhett never left his apartment tonight, or he went with someone before we arrived.

We gave up the surveillance a little after midnight. My eyes wouldn't stay open anyway, so Taylor drove me back home. Every time I think about Rhett's phone calls right after I spoke with Mullins, it makes me mad. I surmise Mullins called Rhett, but I can't prove it, and no judge would sign a search warrant on a sitting Sheriff without indisputable evidence. With the weekend approaching, I vow to myself to follow Rhett one night.

Sleep came quickly after the ruined surveillance, and I never thought about the murders again until I woke the following day. On the drive to the office, everything I have on the case rolled around in my mind. I tried sorting evidence into separate buckets, but nothing worked. The case remains a puzzle I cannot solve yet.

Just as I signed the last overnight report, Braxton Long knocks on my door. I didn't realize how big he was until I saw him stand in my doorway. His shoulders reach out to each side of the doorframe. Braxton stands 6'8," and I couldn't fathom a guess on his weight. Now, I understand why Taylor said we could use him on entries. He would have no problem breaking a door down.

"Good morning, Braxton. Come on inside and take a seat. Maggie has your folder right here with your paperwork. You can use the plastic table over there to complete them."

"Thanks, Sheriff." Braxton walks over to the table and sits in the chair. "I don't think this belongs with my paperwork, Sheriff. It looks like bank records on Rhett Welsh. Are you investigating him for anything? Townspeople say he's bad news."

At that comment, I faced him and asked him what he meant.

"I know Rhett hangs with some dudes over a county. He's some sort of bouncer for a big partier, the last I remember."

"Are you and Rhett friends?" I asked Braxton.

"Friends? No, Sheriff. He went to high school with my cousin. Rhett always skipped school, and he tried to run with the older kids. He was big into drugs for a while. Then the rumors are he got mixed up with heavy hitters over in the next county. I don't know their names, though."

"Interesting, Braxton. Finish your paperwork, then we'll have another conversation, and I'll bring in Taylor." I jotted a few notes on my notepad. Braxton is already helping with the case, and he doesn't even realize it.

Thirty minutes later, Tuttle sticks his head in my office. "Sheriff, do you have a minute? I have someone here you need to meet."

"Come on in, Tuttle. Braxton is here, and I would like to introduce you." The guys shake hands and speak for a minute when Tuttle reaches out into the hallway and pulls a boy into my office. I stare at Tuttle, then the boy, waiting on an explanation.

Tuttle starts his story. "I found this boy on Jose's doorstep. The kid was looking for Jose because Jose gave him football lessons, and he hadn't seen Jose or Margarite in a while. The kid admitted to knowing about Jose and Margarite's side business. He wasn't sure what kind of business it was, but people stopped by their house all the time, and they never stayed long. The kid mentioned Jose and Margarite have a storage unit, but he is unsure of the location. This is the best part. The last time the kid visited Jose, Jose took a phone call from some guy named RT. Jose and RT yelled at each other, and when the phone call ended, Jose threw his phone across the yard and said he could never pay him."

Once Tuttle's story concluded, it stunned me. Who knew a kid would offer so much? Braxton listened to the conversation too. Then he spoke, "Rhett is friends with someone named RT. I'm not sure who RT is, but I suspect he lives in the neighboring county."

"Thanks for bringing the kid by the office, Tuttle. Take him home and come back here. We'll meet and discuss what to do with our recent information."

Tuttle exits with the kid, and we watch the kid look at Tuttle with nothing but questions. The kid knows something happened to Jose, but we didn't share the news. I sat at my desk, and Braxton finished his paperwork. "Braxton, I'm changing your start date to today since you've helped us with the case. We'll get your uniform ordered today, and it will be here in a few days. Here's your badge. Until then, you'll dress in plain clothes."

"Thanks, Sheriff. This means a lot. I'm eager to get started. Let me know where to begin." He stood and shook my hand so hard my elbow hurt. I grimaced, and he dropped my hand.

McAlister called for an update, and while we waited for Tuttle's return, I gave him what information I could prove. His physical therapy sessions are painful, but his range of motion is getting better daily. The doctors are so pleased with his recovery, he might return to work a month earlier than planned. We chatted about the shooter and who I thought it might have been. As we ended, I promised to update him once I knew his shooter's name. When I placed the phone in the cradle, Tuttle popped into my office.

I stand as the crew gathers in my office. We discussed our options after hearing from the kid. Now, we know Jose owed money to someone, or that's the way it sounded. The name RT continued to pop up in conversations, and we agreed we needed his identity.

While in the brainstorming meeting, Braxton asked for the case file. I handed him what I had because I had some things, I hadn't added to the folder yet. Braxton tells the group he will call his cousin and see if he has any information on RT.

"We'll give you a chance with your cousin before we make any more waves. Keep us updated on any information you find." With that comment, I let the crew leave my office. Tuttle is the senior deputy, so Braxton will ride with him today. Taylor stays back for my partner.

Before everyone leaves for patrol, Braxton steps aside to call his cousin. We tried to listen to him talking, but it was nothing more than mumbling from our perspective. He didn't beg his cousin, but we heard him mention RT. Then he waited. Several seconds later, the call ended. "My cousin refuses to be a snitch because he doesn't want to end up like Jose."

"Interesting. Does that mean your cousin thinks RT is capable of murder?" I asked with my eyebrow raised.

"My cousin sounded scared when I asked about RT. He says RT is mean." Braxton shrugged his shoulders as he conveyed his cousin's thoughts on RT.

"I'll make a few phone calls and see what I can turn up today. Tuttle, you'll show Braxton the ropes. Call me later and if you hear any news." Once they left, I called Angela and Ava. Angela was the most believable, but I still have my suspicions about both girls. Angela admitted to hearing the name RT, but the person was unknown to her. Then she pauses as if she has more information, but she sniffs and then ends the call. The call to Ava was like Angela's, as I had a notion both girls were holding out on me. Ava paused when asked about RT. Then she said no, and she didn't explain. If I had to guess, someone was with Ava when I called. At the end of the call, I asked to speak with JoJo, and she told me he wasn't there, then she hung up on me.

With my elbows on my desk and my hands holding my head, I tried to decide how to proceed. Both girls have information, but they are reluctant to share it with me. Should I call Rafael and JoJo? Would they be more forthcoming, or would that make it worse?

Chapter 16

As lunch was winding down, Bud and Lana arrived with our two prisoners. We placed Maria in a single cell and transported Raul to the hospital wing in the jail division. Raul appeared better than I expected after his injury.

While Lana engaged with Taylor, Bud and I discussed the case. I shared the latest news about Jose's friend and the phone call from RT. "Does anyone know RT's full name? He has information we need to solve the case." Bud asked while rubbing his neck.

"No one I spoke with will divulge RT's name. Braxton's cousin says RT is mean, and he doesn't want to end up like Jose. Ava and Angela are hiding something."

"He doesn't sound like a friendly person if he scares these people. Could Ava or Angela have witnessed RT work on someone? Or is he someone's muscle?" Bud asked as he flipped through papers in my folder.

"I'm unaware if they witnessed anything. But they're holding back on me, and that could be why. Moving on to Rhett, would you consider tagging along with me tonight to Rhett's house? If I could follow him, he can lead me to RT."

"I'll go with you because I'll always watch your six," Bud said as he winked.

I straightened my desk as we prepared to leave for home. We needed to grab a quick meal and be back at Rhett's before nightfall. I wanted to see if the apartment remains as it was a few nights ago. If it is, then Rhett is no longer living there. And if he is not there, I don't know where to look for him.

Lana dropped by my office while we were preparing to leave. We spent a few minutes together, and I invited her and Taylor over to my house on Sunday evening. It would give us time to talk about Clement's case. In addition, I wanted to share with her the news article I had written, showcasing the missing items.

Tuttle and Braxton pulled into the lot as we were climbing into my car. I waved them over and introduced Braxton to Bud. They spoke for a minute, then we separated. Bud wants to ride by Rhett's during daylight hours, so we swing by on the way to supper. Since the sun was shining, there was no way to tell if the light was still burning. With Rhett's truck parked in the same space, my fear reemerges that Rhett is no longer living here.

I glanced at Bud, "What happens if Rhett moved from here? How will I find him?"

"We'll get him, Jada. I agree with you. Rhett and RT are players in this case. I'm not sure what role they played in the murders, but they have information to help."

Friday night was a waste of time. No one showed at Rhett's place while we were there. So, we left right after midnight. The light still burned at the doorway, but no shadows passed the windows.

On Saturday morning, it was nice to wake up to the smell of coffee and cinnamon rolls. I leisurely strolled into the kitchen, and Bud was sitting at the kitchen table reading the newspaper. He appeared content with the arrangements. "Good morning, Jada. Coffee is still hot. Grab a cup and join me."

I did just that. I plucked a massive mug from the shelf and filled it to the brim with coffee. There is something about coffee that I can't explain. "Thanks for breakfast. These are yummy. What are you reading?"

"Local stuff. I'm investigating my new home. Things in Georgia are not too different from Louisiana, other than the food. Some food in Louisiana is so spicy, I can't swallow it. Speaking of local stuff, what did you decide about Clement's case?"

"I finished the inventory, and I'm missing two items. The diamond ring I told you about earlier and a gold statue with ruby eyes. Lana and Taylor are coming over tomorrow for supper, and I thought I would get Lana to help me with the news article."

"That's splendid work, Jada. Wonder if the same person stole both pieces? That would be something." Bud nods his head as he imagines someone beating Clement for a diamond ring and a gold statue. How can a person beat another human being to death with a hammer?

"The newspaper and the television will be my best bet on getting the information to the public. I hope it produces the desired effect." My heart clenched as I thought about my dad and Clement and how solving this case would feel.

We spent the day rambling the county roads. I showed Bud things from my childhood, like my schools, the house where Dad raised me, and my favorite diner in the world. The weather is still toasty this time of year, but you feel the seasonal change coming when night comes.

At 8:00 am on Sunday, my phone rings. I cringed as I reached for the phone because nothing good happened this early on a Sunday. The radio static was noisy when I answered, and I didn't recognize the dispatcher's name. So, I had her repeat it. Once I was clear on who I was speaking with, she explained why Sheriff Mullins' dispatcher called me. After her explanation, I sat up in bed.

"I haven't spoken to Mullins since Friday about noon. When was the last time someone spoke to him?" I waited for a reply. "What about his car?" The dispatcher explained his car was missing too. Investigator Davis has been to his house, and it doesn't look like anyone has been home. The newspapers were out on the lawn.

Bud peeks in the door at me with a raised eyebrow, and I waved my hand. He listened to my side of the conversation, but he didn't interject. However, once I ended the call, he was all ears wanting to know what happened.

"All I can say is Sheriff Mullins is missing. No one has spoken to him since Friday after 4:00 pm. One of his investigators stopped by his home, nothing there. They can't find his vehicle either. Mullins sounded fine last time I spoke with him. However, his reason for stopping by was odd. He said he wanted an update on Rhett's surveillance."

With his hands rubbing the back of his neck, Bud asks, "you don't think this has anything to do with Rafael or JoJo, do you? It makes me wonder with all that chatter Mullins referenced."

"I can't answer that question. Mullins seems to be the only one hearing the chatter. My guys haven't heard chatter." But, thinking back over my conversations with Mullins, I question if he was trying to give me a hint with his chatter comments. Did he know something, or does he suspect someone? "I'll call Taylor and have him ping Sheriff Mullins' cellphone. I don't expect any results, but I need to try."

Taylor answered on the first ring, and I explained my call. It took Taylor two minutes to ping Mullins' phone with no results. If a phone is off or the battery is out, it won't ping. However, Taylor told me the last cell tower Mullins' phone pinged from was the area over by the bar where Rhett's shooting took place. I thanked Taylor for his time and reminded him about tonight.

An hour later, Bud and I drove to the famous bar. We scoured the area surrounding the bar, even driving a few unfamiliar roads. There were no unattended car wrecks that we found. In fact, we found nothing. Bud checked the roads for skid marks and car debris, but that didn't help either.

"A cell tower covers a wide birth of land. What is our distance from the bar?" Bud had a pen and paper because his brain always falls back to math. He drew a square in the middle of the paper for the bar, and then he drew lines from the square outward.

"GPS says a half-mile by driving time. Walking through the woods less than that." I offered.

"Drive us back to the bar. I want to check a notion." Bud asked.

While sitting in the bar parking lot, Bud used the car's navigation system to plug in addresses around the bar. He suggested driving a one-mile circumference from the bar. The tower might be larger, but this would give us a fighting chance to find Mullins. One by one, we used the addresses Bud supplied the navigation system, and we came up empty on each attempt.

It's safe to say we didn't locate Sheriff Mullins on the roads within a mile from any direction from the bar. We drove around for hours searching for Mullins with no luck. If he's in trouble, I have no idea where to look. I promised myself I would follow up with Investigator Davis on Mullins's status.

Once we made it home, we prepared for Taylor and Lana's arrival. Tonight was nothing fancy, just grilling hamburgers and hotdogs. The preparation was easy with Bud helping. I've noticed how comfortable he is in the kitchen, and since I'm no chef, his cooking abilities will come in handy.

Later in the evening, I pulled Lana away from the men and showed her my missing items. I thanked her for pointing me to dad's pictures. I found the gold statue in a photo of dad running for Sheriff. Clement grinned big for the picture since it would be on the front page of the newspaper.

Lana reviewed my notes and pictures. "Jada, I can't believe you finished the inventory already. You must never stop working." She smiled at me.

My heart exploded. To find a sister, then almost lose her, then to get her back. How can you not have emotions when she compliments your work ethic? "I stop, but this case means a lot to me. I want to solve it, and I need your help. You mentioned using the media to help locate the missing items."

"I remember. The media can be useful for some things while not so much for others. This would be a prime example of a way they can help." Lana explained while flipping through the pictures. "Clement's store contained a ton of merchandise. Was it always this full?"

"For as long as I can remember, it was full. Some days, his store was so crowded there was no place to stand. Dad sent deputies to control the crowds for Clement. I can still remember dad telling Clement to raise his prices, and that would solve his crowd issue."

Lana laughed at that, but her eyes said something else. Like she missed out on the fun. I haven't pried into her childhood with mom because I don't want to make her mad. But I can't help wondering if her childhood was rough.

Over the next hour, we compiled the newspaper article and the television press release. When we finished, Lana read it aloud to the guys for their approval. Then the four of us chose the pictures of the missing items for the release. The decision for the pictures was more challenging than I expected, but the time was worth it because the result made me proud.

I jumped into Monday with both feet by calling the local television stations first, then newspapers. Everyone I spoke with seemed happy to help me spread the word. Both the newspaper and television stations required an email containing the script and the photos. One elderly lady at the newspaper remembered Clement and offered to run the ad for free, which I accepted.

Before I set the handset down, I dialed Investigator Davis to inquire about Sheriff Mullins. Somehow, I knew the outcome of this call, but I called anyway. Sheriff Mullins' location remains a mystery. No one has seen or spoken to him since late Friday afternoon. We traded cell phone numbers for easier contact.

To finish my morning strong, I strolled to the coffee bar, then to the bullpen. Braxton sits tall in his space, allowing me to see the top of his head. Only two guys sit tall enough for me to see them from the entrance, Braxton, and Taylor.

"Good morning, Deputies. I need to see Deputies Taylor, Long, and Tuttle in my office." With that statement, I turned and walked to my office. Maggie spoke to someone on the phone about a diamond ring. I tapped Maggie on the shoulder, so I didn't scare her. "Send them to me."

As I waited for the call transfer, I couldn't imagine someone already recognizing the ring. When the call came, I knew the caller. It was the elderly lady from the paper. She requested another photo of the ring because the photo I submitted was dark. Once I explained the picture in her possession is the only one of its kind, she agreed to tweak it in a photo editing program. I thanked her for the efforts and ended the call.

Three deputies stood in front of my desk, waiting for instruction. "Take a seat, guys. I need you three to pick up Ava Storie on obstruction charges. I'm tired of getting the runaround, and she has the answers we need to solve this case. Taylor, you'll assist me in the interview room. Tuttle and Long, I would ask that you watch the interview from the viewing room. If you hear anything you question, we need to know it. Knock on the interview room door and then pass a note to us. Do you have questions?"

The deputies glanced at each other and then back at me. "Sheriff, we have no questions. Long you ride with me while Tuttle drives his car. We've never arrested her, so I'm not sure if she'll try to run."

Taylor instructed. Taylor glanced my way, and I nodded my head in agreement. He continued, "meet in the parking lot in fifteen minutes." Everyone turned and exited the office.

While I waited for Ava to arrive, I reviewed the notes on the murders. Dante's threat returns to my brain when I noticed the date of the murder. This is my last week to solve the case, or Dante's threat turns into a promise. I can't let him go after a killer. His mom doesn't deserve that after losing Margarite.

The radio squawked as I listened to my deputy's arrest Ava from her home. Ava tried to escape through the back door, but Deputy Long foiled her attempt. With handcuffs around her wrists, they loaded her into the backseat of Taylor's car for transport.

Long escorted Ava into the interview room and left her alone there while watching her from the viewing room. Ava was a nervous wreck with her bouncing leg and tears sliding down her cheeks. I felt sorry for her in one way, and she made me mad in another. This charade had gone on long enough, and it ends today.

Taylor and I entered the room with water bottles for us and nothing for her. We sat on the same side of the small rectangular table facing Ava. As soon as we walked inside, she started throwing questions at us. We studied her as she continued.

I raised my hand to tell her to stop without having to say it. She complied. "Ava. We get to ask the questions while you answer them. We arrested you on obstruction charges, which carries a sentence of five years in jail and a monetary fine."

"Sheriff, I have obstructed nothing. I swear." Ava pleaded.

"Ava. Come on now. We know you were at the campground the night someone killed Jose and Margarite. We need the details surrounding their deaths, and then we can help you with your charges. Who killed Jose and Margarite?"

"I admit I was at the campground that night, but I didn't see the killing. I had stepped away to the bathroom when it happened. There was a lot of yelling and scrambling when I walked back to the fire."

Taylor asked, "who was yelling? We need names, Ava."

She shook her head from side to side and lowered her eyes. For some reason, she refused to name anyone.

I moved on by asking, "Do you know anyone that goes by the initials of RT?"

Both Taylor and I watched Ava's eyes while she contemplated her answer. "No, I don't."

Her eyes gave her away by allowing a tiny bit of recognition to pass through. She knows him, but she refuses to tell us his name. So we move on to another person.

"Ava, are you and Rhett Welsh friends?" I asked.

"Yes. We are friends, I guess. But he wasn't at the campground that night."

Taylor continues asking questions. "Where was he then?"

"Someone mentioned he worked that weekend," Ava answered, holding her head higher now that she felt better with the questions.

I asked her where he worked, and for an address, then I waited for an answer. She was getting annoyed with us, and I was enjoying it more than I should.

"They said he works at a warehouse job over a county. I'm not sure where it is or what kind of warehouse it is because I've never seen it. I swear."

After an hour of questions, I needed a break. "Taylor, lock her up."

"What, Sheriff? I answered your questions. Why can't I leave?" Ava begged.

"You've given us nothing other than a warehouse that we're not sure if it even exists, and you gave us no names for the murders. I suspect you know exactly who murdered those two kids. So, you can ponder on your future while we continue to search for the killer."

On her way out of the interview room, she looks back at me over her shoulder and asks, "have you talked to Angela? She might have your answers." I didn't acknowledge her question with an answer as Taylor escorted her down the hall to the jail division.

As soon as Taylor reemerges, we convoy to the warehouse location given to us by Ava. Deputy Long rides with me as Taylor and Tuttle follow. It took a while to find the rundown warehouses that Ava mentioned. They sit in the back of a rundown industrial park. The cracked asphalt allows weeds to shoot up from the earth. The further we drive into the park, the more warehouses we find. By the time we go to the rear of the park, there could be ten warehouses.

None of the buildings appear operational. Once we circle the park for a second time, I radio Taylor and suggest we return to the office to do some internet digging. "Deputy Long, what does your gut tell you about these warehouses?"

"If someone uses them, there's a possibility it is illegal. The grounds surrounding the warehouses are unkempt, but that could be by design too. No legitimate businessperson would use a crumbling building for business purposes."

I nodded my agreement. Something is wrong with this picture, and I intended to find out what. Who owns these buildings? That's my first question.

Chapter 17

On our return trip to the office, Long volunteers to find the owner of the warehouses. He admits computers are a passion and will help in any capacity needed. "Thanks for offering your services. Taylor will be grateful for the help too. He's been the sole computer guru for a while now. A few other deputies are learning computer tricks, too, so feel free to share your knowledge with the group."

As I strolled by Maggie, I checked on messages, hoping I had one about the missing items. Even though it was too soon, I had to see for myself. When I turned around, Long stood in my office doorway, waving papers in the air.

"Frederick Upton owns all the warehouses in the name of Upton Holdings, LLC. Upton Holdings is an import-export company per the Secretary of State office website. His only other commercial registration is for his attorney's office. I found no other registrations under his name. Taylor continues digging into Mr. Upton."

"Are Mr. Upton's taxes current?" I asked while I wrote Frederick Upton's name in my book.

"Yes, Sheriff. His taxes are current on the warehouses, attorney office, and personal residence." Long offered.

We looked toward the door when Taylor and Tuttle entered. I nodded for one to talk. Taylor obliged. "Frederick Upton is a high-profile attorney, married with two kids, both in college. No prior run-ins with law enforcement. Not that we expected any."

I rehashed our latest news. "We think these warehouses are where Rhett works from Ava's interview. I don't understand Rhett saying he works at an abandoned warehouse. Long, can you do your computer thing by searching the surrounding area for additional warehouses? Maybe we stumbled onto the wrong ones as Ava didn't give us an address. Although I don't see how there could be space between the ones we found and the town. Between the bar and downtown, there's not much room for a warehouse."

"I'm on it, Sheriff." Long backed out of the room, eager to get started on his assignment.

"I want you two to ask around town about Upton. See if he's on anyone's radar. Since he's an attorney, I expect nothing, but they may offer some insight if someone has hired him as their attorney. I don't want the Sheriff's Office stirring up trouble without reason."

Tuttle nods, and he says, "I agree. Have you considered Ava's comment about Angela? Is Angela keeping secrets from us too?" Tuttle asked with his eyebrow lifted.

With my eyes on my notes, I turned my book around and circled Angela's name in red. "Yes, I think Ava, Angela, Raul, Maria, and Rhett are holding back from us. But I'm hoping since we arrested Ava, word will get around town. And once it does, people will change their attitude toward us and start sharing information."

The guys leave the office for patrol. I reminded them Sheriff Mullins is still missing and be on the lookout. While they were out, I considered my next option for the case. Would Bud stop in on Raul and ask him a few follow-up questions for me? Bud and Lana had a virtual meeting with their Atlanta peers this morning, but the meeting should end within the hour. He'll call or text when he can.

Braxton Long was a superb choice for hire. He joined the office when we needed him most, and he has pushed this case forward. I prayed for the safety of my team every day, and now I added Braxton to the list.

A faint tap came from my door. As I glance up, Deputy Long fills the doorway. "What did you find, Long?" I ask.

"Nothing, Sheriff, nothing. There is no other warehouse on this side of the county. Between the bar and downtown, Upton's industrial park is it. We were at the correct location, but it makes little sense. What can someone do in an abandoned warehouse and then call it to work to their friends?"

I shake my head, knowing I don't have an answer for him. "Taylor is on patrol. If you want to radio him, he can pick you up for a ride-along. If you are comfortable on your own, we'll assign a car to you next week."

The biggest smile so far spread across Long's face. "I'm ready, Sheriff."

As he turned to leave, my cell phone rang. I had the biggest smile of all when the caller told me how much he loved me. Bud knows how to jumpstart my day. I shared with Bud my idea of speaking with Raul, and since Raul is in FBI custody, it would be only fitting for an FBI agent to interview him. The laughter came through the phone. Then Bud agreed to help me. He would come to the office and meet Raul if I agreed to have lunch with him. How did I get so lucky to find Bud?

Bud arrived shortly after our talk, but Raul's doctor visited him, so we opted for lunch first. We talked over lunch about Bud's assignment and then the case. I shared with Bud about the abandoned warehouses we found. His interest showed when I mentioned the likelihood of Rhett working at an abandoned warehouse. "Well, if he works there, it is an illegal business. Have you spoken with Mr. Upton about his warehouses yet?"

I shook my head, "no. I don't want to involve him if I don't have to. We don't need a high-profile attorney suing the county for the unwanted press." I picked up the check, and when I looked down at my radio, Bud grabbed it from my hand and smiled.

"Since I coerced you into lunch, at least let me pay for it." Bud ambled over to the register, and I waited outside. My radio squawked once, but nothing came through.

We drove around town on our trip to the office, and we passed the common area on the backside of the office. Workers were busy replacing the damaged area. In two weeks, the inmates will have a new yard. The county is lucky the fire didn't destroy the office, only the common yard.

In the office, Bud wonders toward the jail division. He and Lana have clearance cards for the Sheriff's Office now. I've considered offering them workspace in the Sheriff's office, but I'm not sure if the county would agree. It would come out of my budget, and I could rearrange it to suit their needs.

I settled into my office while Bud spoke with Raul. Maggie didn't produce any messages, but she confirmed, the newspaper and the news outlets ran the story of the missing items this morning. The confirmation boosted my spirits because this case wasn't moving as fast as I would like. Too many people guarded their secrets, and I couldn't figure out how to break them.

Forty minutes pass, and Bud hasn't returned to the office. Either Raul is talking, or Bud walks the hallways because he doesn't want to see me. I stand and walk over to Clement's board. Every so often, I review what I have on the case. I don't want to sink all my time into the inventory and come up dry. That will be a lot of wasted time.

Bud pops his head inside, and as he turns to leave, he spots me. "I almost didn't see you in the corner. Raul gave us a little information, but I'm not sure how helpful it will be for you."

"Let's hear it." I sat in my chair and laid my hands on the desk. There will be no multitasking during this conversation.

Raul knows Rhett. He didn't say they were close friends, just that they are acquaintances. Raul claimed nothing about a warehouse as he was unsure where Rhett worked or if he worked. But Rhett constantly flashed cash around.

Then Bud moved on to Jose. Raul and Jose were friends, and Maria had introduced them. Maria and Margarite worked together and were best friends. Raul admitted Jose and Margarite were into drugs and worked with him and Maria. Raul and Maria ran to Louisiana because they thought someone would kill them next since they were close friends of Jose and Margarite.

Once Bud felt he had learned all he could about Jose, he moved to RT. When Bud asked Raul if he knew RT, his eyes flickered like he wanted to say something but then chickened out. Instead, Raul turned his eyes downward and rubbed his hands together. Then, just as Bud wanted to ask the last question, Raul's nurse entered the room.

"So, what do you think, Jada? Did you get anything useful?"

"Yes. We did. Now, we know why Maria and Raul ran to Louisiana. It's because they feared for their life. But I still can't put a name to RT. He's the guy who scares everyone. Are Rhett and RT in the drug business or something else? Rhett flashes money around, and RT sounds fearless."

We sat in silence as we added Raul's information to our already packed folder. Finally, Bud leaned back in his chair and linked his fingers behind his head. Then, with his eyebrows bunched, he asked, "did you have your guys look into Upton's children? If both kids are in college, they would be the same age as Rhett, Raul, and Maria. That would explain how Rhett knew about the warehouses."

"I like it, Bud. We haven't looked at the children. Our interest was in the warehouses." I snatched the phone off the cradle and pushed the button for Taylor. He didn't answer his desk phone because he and Long were still on patrol. So, I called his cellphone. He responded right away, and I explained my call. They'll return to the office, and he and Long will jump on my request.

Bud and Lana had an afternoon meeting, so that left me alone in my office. I grabbed a paper and began sorting ideas with specific people. The idea involving all the kids was the most practical. If Bud is right and the kids know each other, they're keeping secrets to protect someone. The someone is RT.

Long and Taylor crashed my thinking with information on the Upton children. The oldest is a son, Chandler, who attends law school in Atlanta. His younger sister, Bethany, attends law school in Florida. Neither child has priors. The son drives a cobalt blue Audi R8 sports car. Bethany drives a Lexus, nothing fancy in hers.

Since I was unfamiliar with an Audi R8, I typed the vehicle into my search engine. "I've seen this car.

But where? It might have been at the bar. If it was the bar, that means Rhett and Chandler know one another."

"Sheriff, here are copies of Bethany and Chandler's driver's licenses. Their addresses are their dad's home address."

"This is interesting information. When Bud and Lana finish their meeting, we'll take a ride to Mr. Upton's house because I'd like to see if Chandler is at home."

Taylor and Long exited my office to return to patrol. I continued stewing over the location of Chandler's vehicle. As I studied the internet picture of the car, I remembered seeing it at the bar the day we drove around searching for the warehouses. The car looked out of place at that bar.

Once Bud and Lana's meeting was over, we took off for Chandler's house. Lana asked about the missing items while we drove, and I told her we had heard nothing yet, but I was still hopeful. Since I wasn't familiar with the Upton's address, I let my GPS tell me when to turn, and as I got closer to my destination, the houses grew in size.

Upon our arrival, the neighborhood comprises only a few houses, and they're exquisite. The exterior is stone, brick and craftsman style with combinations of textures. It took little a brain to see each home is custom-built. Every home in this area is spectacular. The landscaping is breathtaking, with water fountains and circular drives. Flowering trees and grasses adorn most of the lawns, as do ivy beds.

Some lawns have a smattering of metal yard art, while others have none.

When we round the corner, the Upton's home sits on our right. It's situated, so it encompasses the cul-de-sac lot. We had to crane our necks to take it all in because the house stretched from one corner to the next. We located no cobalt blue sports car in the driveway, and closed garage doors obscured our visibility into the garage. Without seeing a vehicle, we assumed Chandler wasn't home.

"I'm driving to the bar. I need to see it for myself." So I continued driving straight out of the neighborhood toward my county. Within fifteen minutes, we cruised past the bar. We didn't pull into the lot because we didn't want to draw attention to us, so I flew past, giving Lana and Bud time to glimpse the cars in the lot.

Lana grunted as she twisted her seat. "I need another pass. There are more cars in the lot than I expected."

"Me too," Bud said as he glanced at me.

"Sorry, I drove too fast for you. I'll slow down on this run." Preparing myself to drive slower, I lifted my foot from the pedal. As I glanced at the bar, I caught a blue flash of color. "Look at the side of the bar. Is there a vehicle backed into a spot?" I asked.

"Jada, you're right. There is a car backed in alongside the bar. Chandler is inside. What's your call?"

Thinking through my options, I wanted to watch the bar. If Chandler leaves, I'm following him. After I shared my thoughts, Lana called Taylor and asked him to pick her up across the street from the bar.

An hour later, Taylor pulls in behind us. He walks up to the vehicle with an idea. "Why don't we send Bud and Lana inside for a drink? No one will suspect them yet. They can scout around and report back their findings."

The bold idea caught me off guard. "Bud and Lana would need to make that decision, not me. They would be in the line of fire if anything came back on their visit." I twisted in the seat to look at Bud and Lana. Both heads nodded in agreement.

"Are you sure you want to do this? If you have the slightest doubt, don't do it." I begged.

Bud raised his hand to shut me up so he could answer. "I, for one, will be happy to grab a drink. This bar looks interesting, sitting all alone on the outskirts of the county. Here are my gun and badge. Hold on to them for me, Jada. I'll be back in an hour."

"Oh, no, you don't, Bud. I'm coming along. Taylor, these are for you."

Bud and Lana pecked us on the cheeks and hopped out of the car. They walked up the street to create distance between us before crossing the road to the bar. The hour they spent in the bar took forever. When they finally emerged, they walked off arm in arm down the street. Several minutes later, they crawled inside my car.

"The bar is small and dark. They play pool, loud music and darts. There was a group of young guys sitting at a round table in the back. One might have been Chandler. I never saw a frontal view, just a side view."

Lana interrupted Bud, "Rhett sat across the table from Chandler. I recognized him immediately. None of the other guys are in your folder. It was too dark to snap photos too."

Bud started again, "whatever they were speaking of was serious. None of the group ever cracked a smile. A few had drinks sitting in front of them, but none ordered repeats while we watched."

Taylor shared a glance with me. We thought alike, and this situation is no different. "Something worries them, or they would enjoy themselves. So, is it something in the past that has them worried, or are they planning a future event?" I stated as I nodded my head.

"Want me and Lana to stay and follow Chandler?"

"Thanks, Taylor, but Bud and I will handle tonight. With the guys being subdued, they will most likely drive to Chandler's house. I'm interested to see if Rhett is staying with him. If he is, then tomorrow, we will pick Rhett up for more questions."

Taylor nodded his agreement. "We'll be ready to grab him, Sheriff. Have a good evening. I have my cellphone with me if you need help."

Taylor and Lana waved as they pulled away from our car. Bud and I settled in because we had no way of knowing how long our surveillance would last. "What do you think happened at the lake, Bud?"

His face contorted into several expressions before he said, "with drugs in the picture, it is likely Jose owed someone money, and he died for it. Margarite, Tucker and Mary Lou were collateral damage. McAlister was too close to shore, and someone shot him to scare him off. Jada, your turn."

"I agree with you, but I'm not sure Chandler is the killer. With him in law school, would he stoop so low to kill someone and risk losing everything? Or is he the mastermind, and Rhett and RT do his dirty work?"

Bud rolled my observations around for a while as we watched a car enter the lot while two exited. Chandler's vehicle remained tucked in next to the bar. "What is Rhett's middle name? Is he the RT?"

That thought never entered my mind. I grabbed the folder and thumbed through multiple pages before I found Rhett William Welsh. A sign escaped my lips as I read it out loud. Bud chuckled. "that would have been bad if RT was sitting right in front of you."

I reached over the console and barely tapped his arm, "don't scare me like that. That would have been embarrassing."

Later in the evening, Chandler exited the bar, with Rhett following. They slid down into the car seats, and Chandler revved the motor as he prepared to pull away. As he exited the lot, he turned right. We had a tough time turning left with the traffic. Lucky for us, Chandler's vehicle is easy to spot. We followed at a distance as Chandler turned into his neighborhood. Once he turns, we passed the neighborhood and drove home.

While driving, Bud and I discuss Rhett's involvement. We agree Rhett is closer to the group than he shares. Bud supported my decision to bring Rhett back to the Sheriff's Office for one more chat. If he doesn't share this time, we can arrest him for obstruction, just like Ava, or at least threaten him with it.

Chapter 18

The following day, Deputies Long and Tuttle transported Rhett to the Sheriff's Office. I let him stew in the interview room for a while. Bud, Taylor and Lana watched the interview from the viewing room. While Long guarded the door, Tuttle sat beside me facing Rhett. Deputy Long can make any man cringe, especially if we make them look up at him. Everything looks more significant from the floor.

Rhett's nerves are doing a number on him. His face reeks of a sweat shine, and he chewed his fingernails. Sweat marks lace his underarms while the room is chilly. My first question threw him a curveball. "Rhett, how do you know Chandler Upton?"

He squirms in his seat, then says, "um, he's a friend from school."

"What school, Rhett?" I throw back at him.

"High school." His eyes shift up and to the right. That's never a good sign.

"You and Chandler met in high school. Have you remained friends since graduation?"

"Well, we're not really friends. We don't hang out together or anything. Chandler is away at law school." As he said it, his eyes shifted, and a finger rushed into his mouth for a few seconds of nail chewing.

A tap on the door brought Taylor into the room. He hands me a note that reads, "Rhett and Chandler did not go to the same high school." I nod as Taylor exits.

"Rhett, let's try again on your relationship with Chandler because I know you did not go to high school together. So, tell me, how did you meet him?"

Another pause before Rhett answered my questions. "I met him through a friend." Rhett barked as he became agitated.

Tuttle shifts in his seat and leans into Rhett's space. "What is your friend's name?"

As he tries to back up, Rhett realizes he can't. "I don't want to tell you her name." Rhett leans over the table and bounces his forehead off it. "I can't believe I said that."

Tuttle and I exchanged a glance and then turned back to Rhett. Time and patience help in these situations because it takes time to wear out the bad guy and patience to put up with his shenanigans.

Again, Tuttle asks Rhett, "Last chance, Rhett. What is your friend's name?"

"Man, I can't say. Ask me another question."

I did. "What can you tell us about the campground murders?" I asked him.

We didn't have to wait for a response because Rhett yelled, he knew nothing about the murders. He continued yelling, "I wasn't there, so you can't hold me on anything. Now, let me go." He puts his hands on the table with his handcuffs facing us as if we'll remove them.

"Sorry, Rhett. You're holding back on us. We'll keep you here until you answer all of our questions." I looked over at Tuttle. "Lock him up."

I exited the room listening to Rhett scream and curse at me, telling me how he would take my badge. I looked forward to him trying.

Bud met me in my office. This case is frustrating because the people involved refuse to snitch on someone else. "Who's the girl that introduced Rhett to Chandler? Is it Ava? The only other girl is Angela, but she's JoJo's girlfriend. So how are Angela and Chandler connected?"

"Is Chandler running drugs for JoJo or Rafael? Is that the key?" Bud offered.

I thought about the drug idea for a minute. "Chandler's dad is a high-profile attorney. Could the boy keep his dad out of his business?" With a head tilt, I didn't see that working. People from all over the county would contact him at all hours of the day and night. His dad will ask questions. "I can't believe this case has been this difficult. Somehow, we must solve this case and soon. Dante will show up at my office door any day now."

"Jada, you can't think like that. If you do, you'll never solve it." Bud walked behind me and rubbed my neck and shoulders as everything fell into place. He's right. I can't consider multiple options if I'm running scared. That's why you learn not to wear blinders when working a case. You have to see all options all the time.

While Bud took a call, I glimpsed my notes again. Rhett's statement bothered me about the girl. In a previous meeting, he mentioned Angela. Is she the key?

I looked up when someone tapped on my door. "Sheriff, I've got something you need to see. Can you walk with me?"

Following behind Long is a little intimidating because I can't see around him, and I like to see the path in front. He ushers me into his desk chair, and I see Facebook open on his work computer. I glanced at him with my eyebrow lifted, and he said, "hold on. It's for work. Look."

Once he taps a button on his keypad, Angela Diaz pops up on his screen. I glance over her page. Then, after a few minutes, I ask Long, "is there any way we can see her friends on here?"

"I thought you would never ask, Sheriff. For your reading pleasure, here it is."

My pulse kicked up when I found Chandler Upton as her friend. The rest of the crew are friends with her too. I followed the trail from Angela to Chandler. On Chandler's page, I found the same friends, along with a guy named Rick. Rick didn't provide a last name. He wanted people to think he's a bad guy as photos show him flexing muscles and lifting weights.

"Did you read this, Long? He mentioned having serious personal issues a day after the murders. I wish we knew this guy's last name. I'd like to ask him about the personal issues."

Then I continued, "I've seen enough. Let's drag Angela in here. Where are Tuttle or Taylor? You can ride with them." I straightened my back and looked over the bullpen. Neither guy was in sight.

"I'll find one. They're here somewhere unless they got called out." Long offered.

As I returned to my office, I found myself hopeful about the recent information. Facebook is a great way to find information on people since they feel the need to share everything with the world. This proves Angela and Ava knew Chandler from the start, but they didn't share his name. Why? We should have our answer to that question soon.

Five minutes passed before the radio squawked, and Tuttle's voice announced he and Long were on the way to Angela's residence. This case deserves a satisfactory ending. Four dead young people in the prime of their lives and one DNR team member shot for what? Drugs or other illegal activity?

Duty calls, so I reviewed reports, handled budget details, and checked in with Grayson in the jail division, all while waiting for Tuttle and Long to bring Angela to the office. While I stood at Maggie's desk discussing Clement's case, Tuttle escorted Angela into the interview room.

Angela's face is solemn. She tried not showing emotion, but it was there, sitting under the surface, ready to explode. Her eyes never wavered as her focus remained straight. Tuttle dropped her in the seat, still handcuffed, and closed the door behind him. I wanted to see how she handled being alone. Would she cry? Would she lay her head on the table?

Tuttle and I entered the interview room after a thirty-minute break. I peppered her with questions, which she answered in one or two words. When I asked about Chandler, everything changed. Angela crumbled. "I dated Chandler, but JoJo doesn't know. Please don't tell him. I've kept that secret for a long time, and I don't know what he'd do if he found out. JoJo is possessive."

"I'm not sure if your dating history applies to our investigation. Ava and Rhett are in jail on obstruction charges. Angela, you're next. All three of you have withheld critical information in this case. Now would be a good time to share whatever pertinent information you have on it, and I may work out a lighter sentence for you."

Angela pondered her predicament, and we waited. Her mind traveled through all probable outcomes, and none of them were right for her. Finally, after a few tense minutes, she succumbed to the pressure. "I'll talk if you let me see Ava."

We stepped out of the room and discussed the ramifications of Ava being a party to the interview. No one found a reason to keep them apart, so Taylor fetched Ava.

Within a few minutes, we gathered in the interview room, which was becoming crowded. Ava and Angela sat on the same table holding hands or as much as possible with handcuffs. I sat in the middle on the other side, and Taylor and Tuttle flanked me while Long guarded the door.

The girls exchanged whispers for a few minutes until I stopped them. "Girls, this is where we are. We have four dead young people and one DNR officer shot. We need answers. Everyone involved in this case knows of the deaths. I want it all, and I want it now. If you cooperate with us, I'll see what I can do about reducing your charges."

Ava spoke first, "if we tell you what we know, we want to be released without charges."

I smiled as I said, "I'll make that determination when I have your information." Both girls turned their eyes down. Angela trembled in her seat, trying not to let a tear slide down her face while Ava worked to soothe her nerves but taking deep breaths. Ava is the stronger one.

"Ava, why don't you start? Tell us everything." I leaned back in my chair and held my pen ready. I expected to learn a lot from her.

We listened as Ava let her emotions take over. She admitted to dating Chandler too. Both girls are friends with Rhett, but neither dated him. Before I asked, they gave us RT's name. It's Rick Tate, and he's the guy who crushed Jose's toes. Once Ava started talking, Angela joined the conversation too. Angela explained Jose owed money to Chandler, and

RT tried to get Jose to pay it back. But he went too far in his interrogation techniques. RT works for Chandler.

We stopped the girls after their last statement. Taylor inquires, "why does Chandler need RT to work for him? I thought he was in law school."

Ava picks up the conversation, "Chandler runs an underground gaming club, known to his patrons as The Club House. RT is his bouncer and collector. Rhett is another bouncer, but he doesn't collect for Chandler. Jose sold drugs so he could gamble because gambling was his addiction. Margarite tried to get him to stop gambling and selling drugs. When he refused to stop, she gave up trying. She loved him more than the fight."

"You're telling us, Chandler, who is a wealthy college student, runs an underground gaming room? Where is this room?" I asked as I tilted my head and raised an eyebrow. It will interest me if they give up the room.

Without a second's pause, Angela offered what we needed. "Chandler's gaming club is in some rundown warehouses on the side of town. They are almost to the bar where Mateo shot Rhett."

"We'll need a layout of the warehouses, and which one holds the games." Tuttle slid a piece of paper to the girls and handed Ava a pen. We let them draw the map, even though we were familiar with the warehouse. Any information they offered would be helpful.

Ava laid the pen next to the drawing. We didn't inspect it because I had one lingering question. My eyes shifted between the girls because the answer to this question would mean more to me than any other.

With eye contact with Ava and Angela, I asked, "who killed Jose and Margarite and Tucker and Mary Lou?"

This stopped the conversation. The girls weren't sure what to say. No one opened their mouths. We waited for the girls to agree on an answer. Finally, Angela gave me what I needed, "RT didn't mean to kill Jose. RT waved his gun in front of Jose as he crushed his toes with a wrench. Jose got mad and fought with RT over the gun. The gun fired, killing Jose. Margarite screamed when the gun sounded, and he shot her point-blank. He said he had to so she wouldn't tell anyone." Tears streamed down both girls' faces as they remembered their friends.

Ava sniffed then continued, "Tucker and Mary Lou walked over to our campground from theirs because they thought something was wrong when they saw us huddled together. RT spotted us talking with Tucker and Mary Lou, and he shot them too. He never asked us what we were talking about. He just shot them. RT dumped all four into the lake, and then he said if we told anyone, he would do the same to us."

We spent hours in the interview room gathering data about Chandler, Rhett and RT. With the information we had, RT is a murderer, Chandler is an accomplice to murder, and is guilty of running a gaming club. This will make the papers for sure.

I thanked them for the information and explained that I would need to hold them for a while—more for their safety than anything. Then, Tuttle walked them back to their cell. He said they never uttered a word on the trip to the jail.

Bud left me several text messages and a voicemail. I called him because I wanted his help on the gambling issue and the case progression pleased him. He asked for a bit of time to discuss the gambling issue with some folks in Atlanta.

Maggie cluttered my desk with messages while I was in the interview. I slid them out of the way so that I could concentrate on the warehouses. The map of the warehouses lay in the center of my desk while I planned the takedown. Five large warehouses sit lined along a road leading from the highway. There are two warehouses on each side of the road, and a more extensive warehouse sits at the end of the road.

As I thought back to our drive out to the warehouses, the road leading to the warehouses is somewhere around a mile long. The two-lane road doesn't have a centerline, and weeds grow from the cracked asphalt. We didn't look inside because we didn't have enough information. Now I'm glad we waited.

Thick forest areas surround the most massive warehouse and the two on the right side, while the other two back up to a large pasture area, which appears to be a sod farm. We don't want to approach the front because they will see us as soon as we turn onto the road. I need to find out what is behind the wood line and enter through the woods.

"Do you know how sexy you are pouring over a crude map of warehouses?" Bud asked with a lopsided grin.

"How long have you been standing there?" I asked with a smile.

"Long enough to hear you ask yourself questions. Now, I'm here to help. Tell me what you have." Bud rolled a chair closer to my desk, planted a soft kiss on my cheek, and took the map off my desk.

Bud studied the map for a few minutes and jotted notes on a pad. We came up with the same ideas. The back and sides of the largest warehouse are our biggest obstacles. The players in the club would run toward the woods to escape arrest. Lucky for us, the players park their cars in the front warehouses. Somehow, we'll lock the doors preventing an exit.

"The FBI agreed to send a group of agents to help with the gaming room. We need to give them an idea of when you plan on doing this raid."

"Tomorrow night is my goal. Tonight, I'm going back to the warehouses for recon. I want to count the cars in the warehouses. That would indicate the number of people in the gaming room. If Chandler's room is large, which has the potential to be, there could be hundreds of people in this warehouse."

"I'm going with you tonight. Taylor and Lana have dinner plans. We'll share our plans with them as a backup." Bud stated. Then he asked, "Has anyone checked Chandler Upton's financials?"

"Not yet. That's on my list, but I haven't requested it. I'll let Long do it since Taylor is getting off soon." I pushed the speed dial for him. He stood in my doorway before I replaced the receiver.

"Come on in. I have a request if you can handle it before you leave. If you can't, we can do it first thing in the morning." I pulled Chandler's information from my stack of papers.

"Sure, I can. What do you need? Thanks for letting me be a part of the interview today. It sounds like you got a ton of information from those girls."

"Yes, we did. I just wish it had been two weeks ago. Anyway, here's Chandler Upton's sheet. Can you run his financials for me?"

"Results forthcoming." Long turns and vanishes from sight.

Chapter 19

His eagerness is contagious. It made me want to go to the warehouses, but I knew I couldn't. All raids take meticulous planning, and we're just beginning.

Deputy Long walked back into my office later with papers in hand. "Chandler is a wealthy individual without his dad's help. He also has an offshore account where he holds gobs of money. Look at these." He placed the papers on my desk for us to peruse.

Bud whistled when he saw the totals in Chandler's accounts. "This is more money than I'll see in my lifetime," Bud exclaimed. "How old is this guy?"

I turned over a page in my folder for his age. "Chandler is twenty-five years old and a multimillionaire. Why on earth would he turn to gamble knowing his dad is wealthy? Is he trying to prove something?"

"Why prove it if you can't share it with anyone? He can't tell people how he makes his money. Does his dad have any knowledge about his money and his gaming club? If so, they'll lose everything." Bud added.

Everyone studied the financial paperwork. Its clear Chandler is intelligent, and he put his brains to work and created a money-making endeavor. It's too bad the endeavor is illegal.

"Can we match Chandler's deposits with Rhett's deposits?" I asked Bud and Long.

"I pulled Rhett's deposits too and highlighted the similar deposits as compared to Chandler's. So I feel sure the cash deposits are from the gaming club." Long explained as he handed the papers to me.

Bud and I nodded in agreement. Rhett works as Chandler's bouncer, and we have proof. We spent a little longer on the financials, then left the office for supper. Neither Bud nor I told anyone about the recon tonight. We plan to call Taylor before we hit the woods as a safety net.

Over supper, we discussed our approach to the warehouses and our goal for tonight. The biggest obstacle we found was seeing inside the warehouses. We need the number of vehicles and an estimate on the number of players, but if they blacked out the windows, we would come away empty-handed. Since this is in Mullins' county, I'll contact his detective division tomorrow about the raid since Mullins remains missing. This will be a mutual aid raid, as both counties will take part. I want Rick and Chandler on murder charges. The FBI can have the gaming club, including Chandler, after I finish with him.

With darkness falling, we sat in a thick grove of shrubs and trees at the forest border. We covered ourselves in black, only allowing the whites of our eyes to show because we couldn't take the chance of discovery. I could still hear Taylor's voice when I explained our night's adventure. However, I didn't know if the tone was because he wanted to tag along, or it worried him. Either way, it bothered me.

At the prearranged time, we approached warehouse two. We numbered them from one to five, starting on the right side. Warehouse three is the gaming club, from what the girls' told us. Warehouses two and four hosted the players' cars.

As we got closer, there was a low rumble emanating from warehouse three. Bud whispered, "air conditioning units," and I nodded my head in agreement. Warehouse two was quiet as we made it to the parking lot. There's nothing to protect us from the wood line to the building, so we run for it. When we touch our backs to the building wall, we breathe deep. We didn't notice cameras on the warehouses, so we prayed we were still in the clear.

We shimmied along the building side. Bud led me to the first window on our side of the building. We didn't want to turn the corner for fear of being seen. They placed the windows in the wall taller than our heads. Bud leaned over and cupped his hands, "climb up there, Jada, and look in the window for us."

I placed one hand on his shoulder and one hand on the wall, hoping to balance myself long enough to get a look inside. "Lift me a little higher, Bud. I can't see anything." I whispered.

Bud strained as he hoisted me up into the air another six inches because that was no easy feat. With the extra height, I spotted the cars. They parked cars nose to tail on both sides of the warehouse. There must be forty cars in there with twenty on each side. There is no way someone could leave early if they parked their vehicle in the middle of that chaos. The warehouse has dim lighting for the cars, and I see no movement or people inside.

When I finished inspecting the warehouse, I tapped Bud on the head so he could lower me to the ground. I described the inside layout of the warehouse with office space upstairs. Bud nodded his understanding. We ran back to the tree line just as a car turned onto the road.

"Do you think they saw us, Bud?" I asked in a panic.

"We'll know soon enough. Although, the car never stopped as it cruised by the warehouse. It continued to warehouse four. I guess they fill up number two first then move on to number four. With the number of cars in each warehouse, if they carry two people each, there might be close to two hundred people inside by the time you add card dealers and bartenders."

"That's more people than I expected. How has Chandler kept this from law enforcement all this time?" I shook my head as I tried to comprehend the size of this case.

"Unless law enforcement is aware of the gaming club." Bud looked at me with a head tilt and creases in his forehead.

"You don't think Sheriff Mullins would cover something this large, do you?"

Bud paused before he answered. "Think about it, Jada. You told me Mullins acted strange a few times. Was it because you were getting close to discovering the club?"

I couldn't answer because yelling came from the rear of the gaming club. We ducked deeper into the foliage as we tried to listen to the issue. Muffled tones were all we could make out, so we slithered through the trees hoping to listen in on the argument. One guy struck another guy in the face with his fist. Then yelled, "you're not welcome here. We don't allow cheaters." Another person appeared and escorted this guy away from the warehouse. After he passed the corner, we were unsure what had happened to him.

We looked at each other. Bud suggested we return to the vehicle. I followed orders. As mad as that guy was over cheating, I can't imagine what he would do to us. The moon was high in the sky when we reached our vehicle, but someone parked beside it. Bud grabbed my arm before I stepped out of the woods. "Whose vehicle is that parked next to ours?"

I whispered back, "the only person I told was Taylor, and that was only for backup, but that doesn't look like his vehicle." I glanced across the area, trying to make sense of the intruder, when my phone vibrated in my pants pocket. Someone sent me a text. I plucked it out of my pocket and breathed a sigh of relief.

"That's Lana's vehicle. Taylor and Lana are waiting for us to come out. He's watching us." I snickered because I knew Taylor would be here somewhere. He is my protector regardless of if Bud is with me or not.

By the time we cleared the woods, Taylor and Lana, dressed in black, holding assault rifles, met us at the back of the vehicle. We shared the information we gathered tonight. Then I had my say, "Taylor, I called you right as we were walking in the woods. I had no intention of you and Lana joining us."

"Sheriff, you of all people know I can't help myself. Anyway, you and Bud survived. Now, we meet tomorrow to put the finishing touches on the raid." Taylor and Lana waved as they strolled to their car hand in hand.

Bud winked at me as we stowed our gear before climbing in the car. "Wonder if Chandler has a cut-off time for arrivals? Also, we have no way of knowing if Chandler will be inside during the raid." With all the unknowns, I second-guessed myself on the raid. My eyebrows bunched together as I revisited the raid idea.

"Are you thinking about calling off the raid? Because if you are, you need to change your mind. Chandler is an accessory to murder, and he runs an illegal gaming room. This guy is bad news." Bud's tone reminded me of why I mentioned the raid. I want both guys. Not only to solve my case but to get them off the streets.

"No, I'm not calling off the raid. But I'm worried it might blow up in my face." Bud started the car and drove away from the woods. As he turned onto the highway, another vehicle turned onto the warehouse road. That proved the gaming club operates into the early morning hours, and our raid will happen long before then.

The next day began with four hours of sleep under my belt. Everyone knew I had little to no sleep, so no one questioned me. Bud appeared the same. The plan began taking shape with all county deputies on duty tonight. Most joining the raid team, while a few will remain at the Sheriff's Office in case of emergencies.

I called Sheriff Mullins again, and still no answer. This time the phone went straight to voice mail, so I assumed his phone was dead. I just hope he isn't. Since I couldn't reach him, I called Investigator Davis. He was apprehensive when I told him about the warehouses. He kept asking if I was sure. I explained about our surveillance last night, and he stopped asking.

When I offered mutual aid in serving the warrant, he accepted. Davis wants to be a part of the takedown, and he'll have his investigative team and some of their deputies join in the raid. We agreed to meet as a team at my Sheriff's Office. The warrant will be available by then too. Then I broke the news about the FBI joining us because of the illegal gaming room. Davis went silent,

"Davis, are you still there?" I asked into the phone.

"Yes, I'm here. Chandler Upton is running an illegal gambling room in one of those rundown warehouses. That's interesting. How did he keep his enterprise quiet? I heard no scuttlebutt in town about it."

"I can't answer, Davis. We'll look for you and your team at one today." I ended the call with a strange sensation in my gut. I didn't offer to share my feeling, but it was there.

Bud finished his call with the FBI as I ended mine. He looked at me and said, "the FBI team will be here by two. They are coming to the Sheriff's Office."

"We'll be ready." I looked back at the map of the warehouses and drew the map on the back of Clement's board. It gave me the avenue to write notes about what we saw and where we saw it. Bud watched without saying a word. When I finished, he stood, walked to the board, and added a few points. We stepped back, studied it, and smiled.

Hunger spoke to us at the same time. "Let's grab lunch, Jada. Then we'll be ready for the meetings."

I agreed and locked my office as we headed out into the parking lot. Just as Bud closed the door, screaming came from the lobby. I bolted down the hall to intervene in the commotion. Bud stayed on my heels, and Taylor met us in the hallway.

When I turned the corner, JoJo stood at the receptionist's window, yelling about Angela. I walked into the room and asked him to calm down. Instead, he glared at me, "I ain't calming down, Sheriff. You're keeping Angela against her will, and you will let her go now."

Bud and Taylor cleared the lobby of citizens, leaving JoJo and me. "JoJo, I'm sorry, but I can't let Angela leave, not yet anyway. She hindered our investigation, and I'm holding her on obstruction charges. I'll make the final determination on charges within the next few days."

JoJo paced around the lobby, rubbing his neck and sniffing. His coat hung further down on the right side, giving the impression something heavy rested inside. My eyes followed his every movement.

He turned, "I'm not waiting." JoJo pulled a gun from his coat pocket and pointed it at my head.

"Come on, JoJo. You're in the Sheriff's Office. Do you honestly think you can pull a gun on the Sheriff and walk out of here?" I opened my hands as a gesture. My goal was to get JoJo to give up the gun, but I wasn't sure that would happen. JoJo might be high on drugs because he acted like he could do anything.

Activity occurred behind JoJo as I turned him to face me at the front door. "I need to lock the door, so no one enters." I reached over and turned the deadbolt. As I did that, I glimpsed Long getting into place on one side of the counter, and Tuttle stood in the doorway on the other side.

JoJo continued to march around the lobby and wave his gun at me. I guess now the county might let me install metal detectors at the front door. I hope it doesn't take a deputy's or sheriff's death to make it happen.

A call came into dispatch, which scared JoJo so much he fired his gun into the ceiling. After the shot, Long subdued JoJo with one punch to his jaw that laid him sprawled on the floor. Tuttle called the jail infirmary, and a jailer appeared with a gurney. They whisked JoJo off to the infirmary first, then to jail. We secured the gun as evidence of the damage and threats.

Bud watched me handle the situation with my guys. He opened the front door once the chaos had settled. "Do you want to make a run for lunch, or can you eat after the fiasco?"

"I'm starving. Let's run out the back door this time. I wonder if JoJo was on drugs. He paced around the lobby like a caged animal."

"Who knows what made JoJo act that way? Deputy Long took care of that situation. I think you should keep Deputy Braxton Long on your payroll. He's already helped since he joined your group." Bud placed his hand on my back and led me out the back door.

When he turned to close the door, he kissed me on the cheek. I turned around and hugged him. The adrenaline is leaving my body, and I'm feeling lethargic. It always treats me like this. Food helps restore my body after a rush.

Over lunch, we discussed JoJo's situation and the raid. With JoJo in custody, my concern falls to the raid. Neither of us found anything missing. The map of the warehouses covers the surrounding area too. We knew the way in without being seen. The XX's on the map signified personnel placement. As long as all the guys showed, we had plenty to cover the area, leaving nothing to chance.

We returned with only minutes to spare. The team had gathered in the conference room, and Taylor entered the Sheriff's Office, waving the signed warrant. I thought the judge wouldn't sign it when we revealed Chandler's father's identity, but I guess that didn't matter in the end. I stood at the front of the room, discussing the desired outcome of the raid with my group.

Davis and his team of twenty entered the room late, but I didn't care. We were together, and that's what mattered most. Davis' group was familiar with the warehouses, but mine was not, so I took a few minutes and pointed out the map. Careful to mention the number of each warehouse since that's part of our communication strategy. Some men drew the map on paper and stuffed it in their pockets.

 My team wore black clothing, with thigh holsters and OC spray on their belts. Each member donned a ballistic vest with Sheriff stitched into the back, and if they choose, they could wear a ball cap with the same logo on it.

Davis advised his group would dress similarly. That will make it easier for the FBI to distinguish the good guys from the bad.

The raid will take place at 1:00 AM. All law enforcement personnel will be in the staging area at midnight, and ear comms will undergo a test first. Then everyone will make their way to their position if no issues arise.

Since no one needed clarification, I ended the meeting. As I glanced at the wall clock, I noticed the

221

FBI team was late arriving. With nothing to do but worry, I sorted my notes again. The FBI team traveling for this operation means a lot to me. I'm not sure if Bud and Lana begged them for their help, but I'm glad they did.

The squawk from my radio grabbed my attention. I listened as deputies advised ten black SUVs entered the lot and drove to the rear of the office. I checked the clock, and the team was only thirty-two minutes behind schedule.

Chapter 20

Bud and Lana met the FBI team outside and gave them a proper escort into the office. With introductions out of the way, we reviewed tonight's plan. It's clear Bud and Lana have a major influence on this team of agents. I stared into the eyes of thirty FBI agents, of which only two were female. Bud never told me how many agents to expect, but I didn't expect this many. We're plenty prepared for whatever happens tonight between the two Sheriff's Offices and the FBI team.

I left Bud and Lana with their coworkers and walked to the bullpen to see mine. Long and Tuttle were in deep conversation when I entered. "Hey, Sheriff." Tuttle acknowledged my presence.

With a head tilt and a raised eyebrow, I answered. "Hey, Tuttle." When I continued staring at them, they felt I needed an explanation.

"We were thinking about tonight. Can Long ride with me to the raid? We figured Taylor would team with you, and Long could team with me." Tuttle's eyes pleaded with me as he waited for a reply.

"I don't see why not? Long, are you up for this? You haven't been with us but a week and a few days, and you need to be comfortable with the raid. Have you taken part in a raid before?" I inquired of Long.

"Yes, in two. Both raids were for drugs. Just tell me what to do. I promise I'll do it." More pleading eyes looked at me.

"Tuttle, it's your responsibility to watch his six at all times. Both of you come home tonight. Long, you answer to Tuttle, got it?" I tried to sound authoritative in my response, but on the inside, I quivered. Could I live with myself if something happened to Long? He's only been a part of our team for less than two weeks. Although, time with the Sheriff's Office means nothing because I'm unsure how I would handle the death of one of my people. The county has been fortunate that they have lost no one since my dad died, and I want to keep it that way.

I watched Long and Tuttle walk off to the locker rooms. They joined the rest of the group in planning mode. They checked their ammo supply, clothes, vest, and whatever else they felt they needed for the raid. Some law enforcement officers are superstitious to the point they carry or wear something special, like a coin, a necklace, or a special picture in their wallet. Where they carry it or how they wear it never changes from raid to raid.

Time slipped away as I watched the clock closing in at supper time. FBI agents surrounded Bud in the conference room. They looked so comfortable sitting there talking. When Bud spotted me at the door, he jumped up and greeted me. The guys looked at me, and they knew the story of how Bud and I met. Bud grinned from ear to ear. "You told them, didn't you?" I whispered.

"I couldn't resist. They asked about the rumors of why Lana and I transferred to Atlanta. So, I gave them the rundown. They approve if that makes you feel better." Bud winked at me.

"You know it does, Bud. I'm here to find out what to do about supper because I can't imagine they want to go to town to eat. We can have pizza delivered if you think that will be okay."

Bud faces the group, "will pizza satisfy your hunger for supper?"

Everyone raised their hands. So, I took orders of what not to order, and anchovies won that round. Over the next hour, I stayed busy with meal prep. Once I called the pizza restaurant, I searched for utensils, plates and soft drinks.

Taylor caught me in my office, reviewing the map on the board. "Hey, Sheriff. How are you?"

I turned and faced Taylor. My soft spot for him grew daily. His concern for me is eternal. "I'm good but eager for the raid to be over. We have so many unknowns and those I can't control."

"We concern ourselves with our guys and let the FBI do the rest. That's why they're here anyway." Taylor stated. He always has a way of making me calm down and see the big picture. I can't control everything, so I only worry about what I can control.

"Thanks, Taylor. You always say profound statements when I need them most. I'm glad you're on my team." We fist-bumped, then he left, leaving me to ponder his statement. My concerns were Rick Tate, Chandler Upton and Rhett Welsh. The rest of the players I could leave to the FBI. Now, my job has become more manageable. Having Taylor on my team is one of God's blessings in life.

Supper came and went, leaving us several hours of downtime. Everyone rested the best they could by calling loved ones and watching television. As time grew closer, the volume of voices subsided while each team member rehearsed their position in the raid.

As I passed the conference room on the way to the coffee bar, I heard Tuttle and Long discussing the raid. Tuttle makes a fabulous trainer. He walks Long through potential scenarios and lets Long share ideas too. I smiled on my way past.

All teams are in place at our prearranged time. Ear comms are in working order, so we'll breach the wood line at the same time when the time comes. Bud and Lana will join their FBI team members. Taylor, Tuttle and Long will be with me.

Rhett Welsch will be our first hurdle if he's working at the door. After that, he'll be an easy takedown. From there, I have no expectations of the number of people inside and how many carry firearms.

I gave the signal for the approach. A line of agents headed straight for the rear of warehouse three. They wanted to secure the gaming club from the back to prevent runaways while the rest of the team made their way to the front.

When we turned the corner for the front of the warehouse, Rhett spoke to another guy, but I couldn't see his face. Taylor crept up behind Rhett and said, "raise your hands and walk to the wall." Then louder, "Put your hands on the wall and spread your legs." Rhett's friend followed Tuttle and Long. They handcuffed him and led him away from the warehouse.

Rhett yelled at me on his way by, "Rick has guns and ammo inside." As much as I wanted to shake it off, his words stirred knots in my gut.

I whispered into the ear comms, "Rick Tate has firearms inside. I repeat, Rick Tate has firearms."

The raid continued, and since Rhett no longer threatened the front door, we walked inside unobstructed. Surprise showed on each team member when they crossed the threshold. Chandler converted this warehouse into a swanky casino. Mirrors adorned the walls giving the place a much larger feel. Chandeliers hung from the ceiling, and a massive bar ran along the outside wall, offering ample room for patrons to enjoy a cocktail. Tucked into the corners were seating arrangements with sofas, chairs, tables and televisions. Also, Chandler's Club House offered a complete menu and player tournaments.

As I turned my gaze upward, I noticed two guys standing on an overhead walkway. They pointed at us, and then one ran to the door at the end of the warehouse. I radioed the activity to the team. The other guy pulled a handgun out of his waistband and fired a shot into the ceiling.

Several team members requested an update over the ear comms. Taylor replied as I watched Tuttle and Long walk deeper into the warehouse. Investigator Davis and his guys headed for the stairs on the left, Taylor and I aimed for the stairs on the right. With the help of a megaphone, Bud announced the raid by telling everyone to remain in their spots until an officer told them to move.

We had several players try to make a break for it, but none succeeded. After Rick fired his gun, he bolted. He shimmied down a pipe on the back wall of the warehouse. When his feet hit the pavement, the FBI gave him a dire warning, which he ignored. Instead, he fired several shots at the officers as he ran to the woods. The agents returned fire and saw Rick fall flat on his face.

Bud stated to other officers in the area, "I'm approaching Rick from his backside. If he twitches, shoot him."

As I waited for Bud's all clear, my heart hammered in my chest, but I continued my job. We found multiple offices at the top of the stairs. They ran the length of the warehouse. After searching the two offices, there was a pounding coming from the next one.

Taylor prepared to open the door for me to enter. When we did, I stopped in my tracks. "Sheriff Mullins, you're alive. Taylor, call for an ambulance. We've got to get him out of here." After he realized who I was, he collapsed onto the floor. Then, I couldn't tell if he was conscious.

"Sheriff Mullins." I prodded him to open his eyes. When he didn't, I said, "We're in the middle of a raid. EMS is on standby, but we can't risk them getting injured. So, hang on a little longer for me." I radioed the teams about Sheriff Mullins. Investigator Davis asked me for my location, and I complied.

Within seconds, Davis walks into the office. "Sheriff Steele, the other offices are empty. I've been told Chandler is on the run. Thanks for finding Mullins."

"Let's go, Taylor. Oh, Davis, EMS is on standby to remove Mullins when we give them the okay."

As we pounded down the stairs, I radioed Tuttle. "Tuttle, status report." When we reached the floor, we turned the corner and ran through the back door. Agents were yelling into the ear comms, but I couldn't decipher the voices because many spoke.

Seconds later, Tuttle responded. "Sheriff, we're in the woods on the right side of warehouse three. Chandler is our rabbit, and I'm uncertain if he carries weapons. Deputy Long is with me."

Taylor and I headed in that direction. As we drew closer to the woods, my cellphone vibrated against my leg. I plucked it out of my pocket and smiled, sending a text with only a heart.

Now, I had to jog to catch up to Taylor. When we reached the woods, I realized it was impossible to see anything in there with our black clothing, and without the moon, there were no shadows. I lifted my arm and grabbed the back of Taylor's shirt. He faced me with his eyebrows raised and his lips apart.

"What's on your mind, Sheriff?" Taylor whispered.

"What do you think about setting up a perimeter around these woods and calling in Rufus? Chandler is our runner, and Rick and Rhett are in custody."

"I like it. We can search for Chandler's car or office for clothing to help Rufus. Call Bud. Get his opinion."

We leaned against a massive tree, and I called Bud's cellphone. Once we discussed the pros and cons, he agreed, it might be safer to wait until daybreak to search the woods since no one knows if Chandler has weapons.

Without a moment of hesitation, I radioed the group through their ear comms. "This is Sheriff Steele. Halt the woods search for Chandler Upton. I repeat, halt the woods search for Chandler Upton. We'll set a perimeter around the woods line, and, at daybreak, we'll find Chandler. Acknowledge my command."

Once the situation softened, I texted Tuttle to meet me at the rear of the warehouse. Taylor waited beside me, and the longer it took for Tuttle and Long to emerge from the woods, the more nervous I got. "Where are they, Taylor? They should have been here by now." I tucked a piece of hair behind my ear and gave it a few twirls with my finger.

"They might have been further into the woods than we expected. Tuttle or Long would have radioed if they needed help. I can't see Chandler taking down Tuttle and Long. Chandler's size wasn't impressive, but Rick was."

My phone vibrated, and I grabbed it. I noticed it was from Davis. They secured the left side of the woods, and my team took the right side. If that's handled, where are Tuttle and Long?

I fired off a text message to both guys asking for a status report. In ten seconds, my answer walked out of the woods. I let out a breath I didn't realize I held. Tuttle strolled to my location with Long following.

"We thought we had him. Chandler crushed limbs as he walked deeper into the woods, but visibility was so poor, you had to creep through the woods. You couldn't see your next step."

"I'm glad you both are okay. Davis' group set the perimeter on the left while our team was on the right. Can you bring Rufus in at daybreak? Long, can help. In the meantime, we'll find something in Chandler's car or office for scent, so Rufus will have it."

Both guys agreed and walked off towards our vehicles. It would be good for Long to see Rufus in action. Who knows? He might like a tracking dog, too, since he's an animal lover.

Taylor and I found Bud and Lana in the middle of securing the gaming equipment. Lana shook her head at the expanse of the operation. "How did a kid get this kind of equipment?"

"I'd like to know that myself. This might lead to something larger if he has ties with another gaming group." Bud's head swiveled on his neck when the sounds of shouting came through the front door.

I trotted to the door with Bud, Taylor and Lana following not far behind. A well-groomed man in his late fifties stood beside a huge Mercedes pointing at the warehouse. Could that be the infamous Frederick Upton?

"Are you Frederick Upton?" I inquired.

He took several deep breaths and lowered his voice. "Yes, and who are you?"

"I'm Sheriff Steele. We're here under mutual aid with Sheriff Mullin's department. Are you the owner of these warehouses?" I asked because I knew the answer.

"Yes, I own them and have for years. So what's going on here? Where is Chandler?"

"Let's step over here so we can talk, Mr. Upton." I ushered him away from the crowd of people that had gathered at his outburst. As we moved, EMS rolled Sheriff Mullins out of the warehouse on a gurney. Mr. Upton's mouth dropped open.

"What happened to Sheriff Mullins?" Mr. Upton asked. "Is he going to be okay?"

"I'm not sure yet. I have a few questions for you. First, were you aware your son, Chandler, was operating an illegal gaming club?" We watched Upton's eyes turn to disbelief.

Chapter 21

"I had no idea Chandler was doing this in MY warehouses. Where is he?" Mr. Upton exclaimed.

"I know it's hard for someone to tell you to calm down at a time like this, but I need you to keep your wits about you until we work this out. We think Chandler is in the woods behind the warehouse. Our deputies secured a perimeter around them, and our search and recovery canine will be here at daybreak to bring Chandler out."

"Sheriff. You must believe me. This operation is foreign to me. Chandler is in law school in Atlanta, not down the street, running a gaming room. Can I go inside?" Mr. Upton pleaded.

"No, sir. It's a crime scene now. The FBI is handling the gaming club. We're arresting Chandler for conspiracy to murder."

"You what? There is no way he killed anyone. I'll sue you and everyone out here. You know I'm an attorney." Mr. Upton puffed his chest out so I would cower.

"We're investigating four murders at the campground, and we stumbled on the gaming room. His bouncer, Rick Tate, is the shooter, but Chandler was there for the shooting. He helped in the body disposal." Again, Mr. Upton received more bad news, from his warehouses being used as an illegal gaming room to his son being charged as an accessory to murder. His face showed the emotional toil this put him under.

"I need to sit down. I'm not feeling too good." Taylor ushered him to the hood of a patrol car. Mr. Upton leaned on the vehicle and lowered his head while he rubbed the back of his neck. "I've never been so shocked. Is there a chance you are mistaken about Chandler and the murder charges?"

"No, sir. No chance at all. We'll bring him out to you in the morning. You're free to remain here, but you must not attempt to enter the warehouse. We'll arrest you." I turned and walked toward Bud.

Bud and I discussed the warehouse. The amount of money sitting in a safe on the upper floor is staggering. Greed is a killer, no doubt. The more money you get, the more you want. If Rick had not started the process by killing the kids, the gaming club could have gone undetected for years.

"This is for Rufus. It's Chandler's monogrammed button-up shirt." Bud handed me a bag with the shirt tucked inside. He kissed me on the cheek, then turned and walked off. "See you later, Sheriff. I'll join the search when I can."

He left me standing alone, staring at the woods. In a way, I felt bad for Frederick Upton, but in another way, I didn't. Apparently, he left Chandler alone to handle life, but instead of following in his dad's footsteps, he stepped out on his own. Chandler decided running an illegal gaming club would be better than law school. Life is all about choices, and I guess Chandler made his.

Tuttle radioed me and advised he was entering the road for the warehouses. Rufus barked because he was ready to show us his stuff. I laughed because Rufus has the sweetest face of any dog around, and I carry dog treats in my car just for him. After the bark, I replied to meet me in the rear of warehouse three.

I motioned for Taylor to follow me because I wanted him to be a part of the woods search. "Tuttle is on his way. We're meeting in the rear lot."

"Great. Let's go. I can't see a guy like Chandler feeling too comfortable in the woods. He looks like a city guy. With Rufus on his tail, it shouldn't take too long to find him." Taylor said as we headed back into the woods.

Both Sheriff Office deputies took up positions around the tree line. We could have used more people, but we worked with what we had. Investigator Davis found me as I approached Tuttle and Long.

"Sheriff Steele. A moment, please." Davis asked as he stepped away from the group.

"Davis." I nodded to get him talking. Chandler was my pressing priority.

"Sheriff Mullins expresses his gratitude. He is dehydrated but otherwise okay. He would like for you to stop by the hospital when you can. The doctors are keeping him for a few days for observation."

"Sure. But right now, I have a criminal to capture. Excuse me, Davis." I started back toward my guys.

Investigator Davis trotted up beside me. "I'm here for you. Point me in the direction."

"Follow me. We're entering here. From there, it's up to the dog." I handed Tuttle the bag I carried with Chandler's shirt. Rufus barked when he caught a whiff of the shirt.

Tuttle leaned into Rufus, and they talked a second. Rufus sat in place while Tuttle placed Chandler's shirt in his face. Rufus sniffs, then takes his nose away from the garment, then sniffs it again. This time he let out a bark. That's his sign of readiness.

With the leash wrapped tight around his hand, Tuttle, Rufus and Long led the way. The rest of us fanned out so we could cover more ground. Everything was going well until we reached a small creek. Rufus sat down beside the stream and drank water. The trail stopped. Tuttle leaned into Rufus and said something no one understood but the dog. Rufus lifted his head and sniffed. He followed the wind.

We crossed the creek, then hiked a slight incline. Rufus stopped at a broken tree. We scanned the area finding drops of blood. "Can someone mark this for the crime scene unit?" I said as we continued. Now, what kind of injury does Chandler have? I don't remember seeing it happen to him on his way out of the warehouse.

Rufus picked up speed at the top of the hill. He's on to something, and I hope it's Chandler. If we don't find him soon, he'll have made it to town. Of course, anyone driving by would be obliged to give the kid a lift.

I spoke into the ear comms. "Davis, bring your guys eastward toward the middle. We need to cut him off, and we're heading northeast. Rufus is onto something now."

Rufus stopped short at the base of a small hill and acted as if he had found Chandler. However, I saw nothing. "Tuttle, why did Rufus stop?" I pointed to the dog.

"He found him, Sheriff. He's in there." I followed Tuttle's hand, and he pointed to a cave entrance. Everyone backed up when they saw what Tuttle was pointing out.

I motioned for everyone to gather at the side of the cave. We discussed the cave, and no one was aware of its existence. "I'll try to talk him out. He must be tired and hungry."

"Chandler Upton. This is Sheriff Steele. We know you're in there. Come on out so we can talk." I waited and waited and nothing.

"Chandler. Don't make this worse for yourself. Your dad is waiting for you at the warehouses. He's worried sick about you." Again, I waited. This time I heard movement. Was Chandler coming out?

"Lady. My dad doesn't care about me. He only cares about himself. Try again. I find no reason for me to come out. Why don't you send someone to get me?"

I stared at my feet. Chandler felt like an unloved kid, and we took away his favorite toy. That is a complex emotion to overcome. Every kid wants their parents to love them, but some parents buy the kids love, and some give time because they don't have money. Chandler's dad had the money but not the time.

"Chandler, if I send someone in to get you, there might be injuries. Come on and walk out. We can get you something to eat and look at your injury. We found your blood trail."

Nothing came from the cave. We stood in place, looking at each other, trying to find an alternative way to get Chandler out of the cave. Then, someone approached us from behind. We turned and aimed our weapons at the intruder. Mr. Upton walked up to our location with his hands in the air.

"Can I try to talk him out?"

I nodded because I didn't have an option. No one offered another way either. So, why not let the dad talk him out? Before Mr. Upton started begging, Tuttle and Long escorted Rufus back to the car.

The group stepped back and gave Mr. Upton space. I'm not sure how he expected to make amends to his kid from outside a cave, but at least he'll try.

Exhaustion took hold of some guys as they sat on the ground in the shade and rested while Mr. Upton pleaded with his son. A few guys even squeezed in a power nap. I was never one for a power nap because my naps were full-blown two hours naps.

Forty-five minutes into the cave chat, Chandler walked to the entrance with his hands up. One hand was bleeding, and it ran down his arm and dripped onto the ground. Taylor pulled gauze and tape from his backpack and walked up to Chandler.

Chandler held out his hand to Taylor. "Is this a gunshot, Chandler?" Taylor looked back at me and nodded.

I trekked my way to them and inspected the injury. It sure looked like a gunshot wound. There was a perfect hole in the palm of his left hand. "What happened, Chandler?"

"When Rick slid down the pipe to escape, the gun fell out of his waistband, and when it hit the ground, it fired a round. I was running past at the time. The bullet hit me in hand." Chandler looked defeated. His clothes are filthy, and his eyes are red-rimmed.

"Come on. Let's get you cleaned up and something to eat." Chandler walked between me and Taylor with Mr. Upton on my other side. It was a solemn walk back to the warehouse since we had been awake for hours. Now that we captured everyone involved, it's time to put a bow on this case.

Chapter 22

Taylor escorted Chandler into the jail division, where Grayson took over the duties. He fingerprinted Chandler and placed him in a solitary cell, away from Rick Tate. I didn't want anyone in the group to be close to one another. The girls, Ava and Angela, were an exception. They helped solve this crime spree.

Once I checked in with Davis and my group and noted no injuries, I sent everyone home. Taylor tried to talk me into staying for Lana, and I declined. I went home too. Bud knew where to find me, and I'm sure Lana did as well.

The day after the arrest, I stopped by the hospital to visit Mullins. I wanted to get his story firsthand because I wasn't sure if I could believe whatever he said, anyway. Mullins was drinking juice when I entered his room. "Hi, Sheriff. I need to ask you a few questions if you're up for it."

He swallowed his last swig of orange juice before speaking. "Sure. I'm not going anywhere yet."

Mullins gave me the rundown of what transpired in his detainment. He said he went to the warehouses and peeked in through a window when a large man wearing a ball cap struck him over the head with something. He blacked out, and when he awoke, he was in the office. Someone had bound his wrists and his ankles with duct tape and left him unattended in the office. They never returned to check on him.

Mullins carried on about not having food and water for days. He spent his time kicking the floor, hoping someone would hear him, but the music was always loud.

I took notes, but Mullins couldn't identify the guy who slugged him, other than the ball cap. So, Mullins didn't help my case any, but he didn't hurt either. We can tie Chandler and Rick to this assault too. Their charges keep growing by the day.

As I left the hospital room, Mullins asked me for lunch because I saved his life. I declined and kept walking.

The media met me at the Sheriff's Office. I wasn't ready to provide a press release yet, so I asked for a few hours to prepare. We scheduled the news conference for 1:00 pm.

Bud and Lana showed up around ten. Both looked tired but glad the raid was over. We completed reports in triplicate for all the departments that contributed to the raid's success. It made me proud not one deputy or FBI agent sustained an injury. The FBI confiscated bundles of money, and I captured my murderers. While Bud finished, I stepped outside the office to call McAlister.

"Hey, McAlister, it's Steele. We arrested your shooter last night." We continued talking for a while, and he thanked me multiple times for calling. As soon as he completes rehab, he'll be back in action. I was proud of him because I'm not sure how I would handle it if someone took away my job.

Now, I wanted a huge lunch then to conduct the news conference. I've invited the FBI to attend, but I haven't received a response. This outcome should help the county realize how valuable the FBI can be and allow the Sheriff's Office to offer workspace to the Feds. But, of course, they will be here anyway since Taylor and I work here.

I walked into the office as Bud and Lana stapled their reports and slid them into a folder. "Let's go, guys. I'm starving. I have to be back for the news conference."

Bud grabbed my hand. "You'll be the best-looking person on the stage." He winked as he kissed me on the cheek.

"So, who from the FBI is joining me on stage?" I asked with a lifted eyebrow.

"I will." Turning, I looked at Lana. She grinned from ear to ear.

"Two sisters on stage for the world to see. Who would have ever thought?" I hugged her, and the three of us exited the office for lunch at my favorite diner.

While we waited for the food, I jotted notes on napkins. If I could talk myself into not using the napkins, I'd have part of my speech written. Unfortunately, my notes seem to disappear if I don't make them in my book. I end up leaving them somewhere, or they slide into a file, and I never see them again.

Bud and Lana helped me write the news release because I didn't want to forget anyone in the raid. The public deserved to hear the details of what happened. As bad as I hated to do it, I would announce charges for Chandler and Rick at this press briefing, including McAlister's shooting, which will increase Rick's charges.

As the press briefing neared, I added a touch of makeup to not appear so washed out. Unfortunately, the long hours didn't help my complexion, and the cameras won't be of any help either. The lobby is at capacity, so I walked out the side door of the office and entered through the front. With a crowd this size, we'll move the news conference outdoors.

With two index fingers in my mouth, I whistled as loud as my lungs allowed. The crowd turned my way. I said with a smile, "please move outside onto the sidewalk. This group is too large for the lobby. We'll start at 1:00 pm."

I walked away from the lobby area, headed to my office. As I turned the corner, I noticed my door was ajar. With caution, I pushed the door open enough to glimpse inside. Nothing appeared disturbed, so I went to my desk and gathered my notes for the news briefing. Was Maggie in my office, or did the door not latch earlier?

When I stepped up the bank of microphones, questions flew at me from all directions. Lana stood beside me, looking like a professional FBI agent. I raised my hand to quieten the group. Then I inhaled once, and the news release took on a heart of its own.

The news release provided the group with a rundown of events from the lake recoveries of all four victims, the McAlister shooting, and the gaming club. The reporters remained quiet through the ordeal. They didn't want to miss a piece of information. In the end, the reporters asked questions of Lana and me. The most troubling question referenced Tucker and Mary Lou and their involvement with the criminals.

"Tucker and Mary Lou was at the wrong place at the wrong time. Mary Lou heard Ava talking at the next campground and feared for her safety after the gunshot. So, Tucker and Mary Lou walked over to Ava's campground to check on her, but they stumbled onto something much larger. Rick Tate killed Tucker and Mary Lou to keep them quiet since they knew about Jose and Margarite's murder."

There were a lot of gasps and ohs coming from the crowd. The next question referenced Frederick Upton and his son Chandler. The reporter asked if Frederick was involved in any of the shenanigans at the gaming club. Lana answered, "Other than owning the warehouses, none that we are aware of yet. But we are still investigating the possibility."

Once we answered the reporter's questions, we called it quits. I sighed when I entered my office because being on camera is constant emotion, and that's not for me.

In an agreement with the FBI, I got to charge Chandler with accessory to murder first. Then they get to have him on illegal gaming. Chandler had almost a million dollars stashed in the safe at the warehouse, plus the money on the tables. The FBI arrested 103 players, 45 gaming club workers, and six bartenders.

Overall, we considered the raid productive and an excellent joint operation between the three departments. However, as I closed the folder on the raid, I noticed a message on my desk, and my heart fluttered.

Chapter 23

The message was from Juanita with no last name, and she wanted to talk about a diamond ring. I dialed Juanita and listened to the phone ring five times. As I was giving up on her, she answered like she was out of breath.

"This is Sheriff Steele calling for Juanita."

Juanita introduced herself too. She said she had information on the diamond ring and would like to meet me alone. So, we set an appointment for the following morning at ten. She agreed to come to the Sheriff's Office for the meeting.

Anticipation coursed through my body as Juanita and I ended our call. I texted Bud right away because I was unsure if the FBI de-brief had finished. While I waited on a reply from Bud, I stood at the board. I flipped it over, and Clement stared at me. With Juanita's meeting tomorrow, many ideas ran through my mind on how and why someone killed Clement over a ring and a statue. But I knew for certain Clement's death was a waste.

Later that evening, Bud and I discussed a few reasons Juanita asked to see me in private. Some were logical, while others were farfetched even for two seasoned law enforcement officers. Tomorrow would give me the answers I so desperately wanted. Trying to sleep proved harder than expected after the last two days.

The clock ticked ever so slowly as I sat with my arms resting on the edge of my desk. My leg bounced under my desk, giving way to my nerves. When our prearranged appointment came and went, I thought Juanita changed her mind. But a few minutes after ten, she entered my office carrying a bag over her shoulder with her head down and unshed tears in her eyes.

"Hi, Juanita, I'm Sheriff Steele. Please have a seat." I said with a smile. Before returning to my seat, I closed the door to the outside world.

"Hi, Sheriff. I guess I'll explain my situation." She looked down at her left hand, slid a diamond ring off her finger, and then laid it on my desk. "My boyfriend, Jerald Travis, gave me this ring as an engagement ring. I've always wondered how he could afford something so grand. But then, he gave this statue to my mom on her last birthday on earth." The tears ran down her cheeks in a steady stream now. I placed a tissue box in front of her and gave her a moment to settle herself.

"Juanita, where is your boyfriend?"

"That's the thing, Sheriff. He's in prison and has been for years. We're planning on a Christmas wedding since he gets out in November. Please tell me these are not your missing items." Juanita's eyes begged me for a pleasing answer.

"I'm afraid they are, Juanita. Both items are from Clement's store." My words crushed Juanita, and she crumbled, sitting in my chair.

247

I walked around to her and placed my hand on her shoulder. "I'm so sorry for your troubles. Why don't you keep the items and let me do some digging on my end?"

"What are you going to do, Sheriff? Will I get Jerald out of prison?"

"Juanita, I will not sugarcoat the issue. If Jerald killed Clement, we would try him for murder. I have evidence of the killer's fingerprints, so I'll ask for a comparison and go from there."

"I understand. Thank you for meeting me. Are you sure I can keep the ring and the statue for now?" Juanita's mouth spread into a slight grin.

"I don't see why not? Clement's family is deceased, so there is no reason to take the items from you. If we go to trial over the murder, I'll request the items from you as evidence. Please don't leave town without my knowledge, and I'll stay in touch when I have more information."

We parted ways at my office door. I felt relief knowing where the items went when the killer stole them. But on the other hand, I was mad that no one found out sooner. I marched over to Clement's evidence box, and I rummaged around in it until I found the hammer. I placed it in my carry bag so that I could deliver it to the crime tech. Harold would be perfect for this case.

I called Harold on my way over to his office. Doc James answered, and I explained my situation. He and Harold are both on duty and will await my arrival.

Both guys sat behind a table, eager to get their hands on this hammer. "Gentlemen, nice to see you. I need the fingerprints from this hammer compared to the prisoner, Jerald Travis. He's currently incarcerated in Jackson."

"Is this Clement's hammer?" Doc James asked as he looked it over.

"Yes, do you remember his murder? I inquired.

"No. I wasn't here yet. I remember your dad talking about it, but he never had a solid lead." Doc James explained.

Harold asked to look at the hammer. He pointed to an area of the hammer and said, "there is still fingerprint powder on it. There should be prints in our file somewhere. Give me a minute, Sheriff. We might not have to dust it." Harold stood and walked into the storage room. He opened and closed multiple file cabinet drawers. Then silence as he walked back into our room.

"Here they are, Sheriff. Let's pull up Jerald's and see if I can give you a preliminary match." He said with a smile.

While Harold and Doc James conferred on the fingerprints, I paced outside the office. How will I handle this if they match? I want Jerald Travis charged with murder because Clement deserves it, but do I let Juanita keep the ring? My insides twisted in knots as I awaited the results.

My cell phone rang, and I plucked it out of my pocket. I didn't want to answer because Harold's results were forthcoming, but the caller was Maggie. "Maggie, what's up?"

I listened as she explained Dante waited for me in the lobby. She said he refuses to leave until he sees me. "Maggie, explain to him I'm in a meeting with Doc James, and I'll be there as soon as I finish." Then I wondered about Dante's reasons for wanting to see me. He should be grateful we caught Margarite's killer.

My pacing eased as I tired. Then, just as I sat, the door opened, and Harold waved at me to follow him. Doc James stood behind a table, waiting until we joined him. "Okay, guys, I can't stand the wait. Do you have a match?"

Harold grinned, "yes, Clement's killer is Jerald Travis. We matched multiple prints, so there is no doubt."

I couldn't decide if I should jump up and down or cry, so I did neither. "A big thank you for your help on this. It means a lot to me." Leaning over, I shook both of their hands and headed to the office to face Dante.

I should have scooted along to the office with Dante waiting on me, but I didn't because I wanted time to process the case findings. Jerald Travis killed

Clement. Why? Was it for the diamond ring and statue? I needed an answer.

Maggie was right. Dante still sat in the lobby when I walked through the front door. However, he stood when he saw me enter. "Sheriff, I just need a moment." I waved at him to follow me.

We entered my office, and once he cleared the door, I closed it. "Hi, Dante. What can I do for you?" I asked with a half-smile.

"Mom and I thank you for what you did to find Margarite's killer. I apologize for threatening you." Dante lowered his head as he said his peace.

"Threats don't work on me like they do others, Dante. I did my job, and that's what it's all about to me. Thanks for coming to the office. It means a lot." I said with a smile as I extended my hand. He took it, and we shook hands, then he exited the office.

My desk remained cluttered with messages that had been there since the raid. They need a return call, but I wanted to finish Clement's case. So I called Jackson State Prison and spoke to the warden explaining my situation. He granted me a visit with Jerald and his attorney. We scheduled it for one tomorrow afternoon.

For two hours, I worked on the questions for Jerald and what I planned to accomplish with this meeting. My pad of paper only held two questions. First, why did you kill Clement? Second, are the diamond ring and the gold statue the only items taken from Clement's store?

Clement's case file contained a multitude of photos. I chose a few from my board and two from the file. Jerald Travis needed a reminder of the crime he committed, and I would be the one to give it to him.

Bud tapped on my door before barging inside. "Bud. I'm finishing up for the day. I'm leaving early in the morning for Jackson. The warden allowed me a visit with Jerald Travis tomorrow afternoon. I want to look at him in the eye and show him the pictures of Clement's body."

"I'm going with you. Maybe the warden will let me accompany you into the interview room. Prisons are creepy, even for me."

"I can't ask you to do that, Bud. You and Lana have your own agenda. I don't need babysitting all the time." A wink brought a smile to his face.

"Humor me, Jada. It would make me happy to travel with you tomorrow."

"Okay, I give. It's a date. We leave at eight with the meeting at one. Then a return trip tomorrow afternoon. My interview will be thirty minutes. I have fingerprint evidence Jerald killed Clement." I pointed to Harold's report.

Bud reached over the top of the desk and lifted the report to his face. He studied it for a few minutes, then placed it back on the folder. "You're right. You got him."

"Let me tell the group I'll be out tomorrow but should be back by late afternoon. Follow me."

We strode hand in hand to the bullpen. I shared my news, then Bud and I went home to relax. The last few days have been stressful, and I was glad they were behind me. Now, my focus is on Jerald. With my evidence, Jerald might confess, which will take a trial off the table if he does. I don't want to put the county through a cold case trial if it's not warranted.

The sun was shining when we left town on our way to Jackson State Prison the following day. I drove Bud through the south Georgia countryside. The roads took us by small roadside markets and some long-forgotten motels.

Bud was right about prisons. They have a whole distinct feeling compared to a county jail. The smells, the testosterone, and the sounds made this place creepy. We passed many locked cell doors to reach the interview room. A guard escorted us the whole way, and for that, I was thankful.

The guard led us into a small square room with poured concrete walls. A metal rectangle served as our table with two chairs on either side. Bolts secured the table and chairs to the floor. The warden entered after we did, and he introduced himself to us. A guard, Braxton Long's size, escorted Jerald Travis and his attorney into the room.

The warden stated the procedures and turned the meeting over to me. I was ready. After I introduced myself again, I mentioned Clement's name. Jerald Travis went rigid. He didn't fidget, and he didn't blink. His eyes never wavered from the wall behind my head.

My first question was, Why did you kill Clement? Jerald's attorney tried to stop him from speaking, but he encouraged the conversation when I showed him the fingerprint proof. Then, his eyes shifted to mine and never left as I listened to Jerald tell me his story.

Jerald was a young boy, and Juanita was his first and only love. They had discussed eloping because neither set of parents thought they should marry at such a young age. Since Jerald didn't have any money, he went looking at Clement's store for a ring. He ran across the diamond ring, and he knew he must have it, but the only way to get it was to steal it because Jerald didn't have a job.

His story continued by saying he didn't mean to kill Clement. The hammer was the only thing he had with him. The theft was unplanned. It just happened when he drove by, and Clement was leaving the store alone. He just wanted the ring for Juanita, but as he passed by the shelves, he spotted the statue and thought of Juanita's mom. He thought if he gave her the statue, she might agree for Juanita to marry him. Jerald claims his love for Juanita to this day.

After Jerald's confession, I advised them we would charge Jerald with murder, and since he confessed, there would be no need for a trial. Jerald's attorney agreed, and we ended the meeting.

Now, sitting in my car, the tears rolled down my face. I couldn't stop them. Dad's only unsolved case is no longer unsolved. It feels like I closed another chapter for dad.

Bud didn't stop me from crying. He just held on until they quit. "Your dad would be so proud of you. You finished his unsolved case. Now, he can rest peacefully knowing Clement can too."

Since I didn't have any words, I backed the car out of the space and headed home. My thought lingered around the murder board. I wanted to get to the office and finish what I started. The drive home was quiet. Bud seemed to enjoy it too.

When I entered my office, I walked over to the board, pulled off Clement's pictures, and tucked them back into the same evidence box. As I closed the lid, Bud walked in and hugged me. "Come on out to the bullpen. We're sitting around discussing the case."

Bud wasn't kidding. Lana, Taylor, Tuttle and Long sat in the bullpen, rehashing the case's outcome. Everyone agreed that Tucker and Mary Lou were in the wrong place at the wrong time. Rick did the deeds by killing Jose and Margarite first, with Tucker and Mary Lou following. Rick also shot McAlister when he felt McAlister was too close to the campground, and the ballistic test proves this. We charged Rick with multiple counts of murder and aggravated assault with a weapon. He may never see the outside of a prison cell.

We charged Chandler with an accessory to murder and operating an illegal gaming club. His dad retained a high-profile attorney out of Atlanta to represent Chandler, but with our evidence, he'll go to prison too.

Mullins is the lingering question. Unfortunately, we can't prove his involvement in the gaming club, but I still have my doubts.

Then, to top it off, Clement's case was solved with Lana's suggestion of using the media. Finally, we charged Jerald Travis with the murder of Clement Locke. I haven't spoken to Juanita yet. Her plans of having him home for the holidays are gone.

We listened to a cell phone ring, and Tuttle answered. His face broke out into a smile, and he blushed as he listened to the caller. We clapped now that Tuttle could make time for his new love interest.

The group sat around and talked a while longer. We've been so busy. It's nice to see Braxton spending time with his peers.

Just when we thought we could rest, the radio squawked.

Other Books by A.M. Holloway

Mission: Murder (Ryker Bartley Mystery Book 1)

Murder for Justice (Digger Collins Thriller Book 2)

Flames of Murder (Mac Morris Thriller Book 2)

Promises of Murder (Sheriff Jada Steele Book 1)

Pieces of Murder (Digger Collins Thriller Book 1)

MOA (Mac Morris Thriller Book 1)

~~~~~~~~~~~~~

Visit www.amholloway.com for new releases and

to sign up for my reader's list or simply scan the
code.

91080699R00144